D1600432

RIDE FOR JUSTICE, RIDE FOR REVENGE

Center Point
Large Print

Also by James J. Griffin and available from Center Point Large Print:

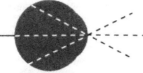

**This Large Print Book carries the
Seal of Approval of N.A.V.H.**

RIDE FOR JUSTICE, RIDE FOR REVENGE

A Texas Ranger Luke Caldwell Story

James J. Griffin

CENTER POINT LARGE PRINT
THORNDIKE, MAINE

This Center Point Large Print edition
is published in the year 2022 by arrangement with
the author.

The text of this Large Print edition is unabridged.
In other aspects, this book may vary
from the original edition.
Printed in the United States of America
on permanent paper sourced using
environmentally responsible foresting methods.
Set in 16-point Times New Roman type.

ISBN: 978-1-63808-357-3

The Library of Congress has cataloged this record
under Library of Congress Control Number: 2022933069

Foreword from Robert Hanlon

This new adventure from James J. Griffin introduces a Texas Ranger you won't want to forget. Luke Caldwell is, if I were to pick, the next big series—he's tough, realistic and completely likeable. This character should satisfy all the readers who have enjoyed the new wave of Western series currently pleasing readers around the world. If this book isn't a popular choice, I'll be a monkey's uncle.

Robert Hanlon, bestselling author of
"Timber: United States Marshal"
and many others.

RIDE FOR JUSTICE, RIDE FOR REVENGE

Chapter 1

Texas Ranger Lieutenant Luke Caldwell pulled Pete, his tobiano paint gelding, to a halt. He raised his right hand, ordering the six men strung out behind him to also rein in.

"Gather around, men."

The rest of the Rangers in his patrol, a detachment out of Company D of the Frontier Battalion, moved their horses into a semi-circle, facing him.

"What've you got, Luke?" Sergeant Ben Thibodeaux asked.

"It looks like we've reached the end of our chase. Those *hombres* we've been trailin' for the past ten days have ducked into Seminole Canyon. There's only three ways out of there; right back out the way they went in, a hard climb through Presa Canyon, or swimmin' across the Rio and into Mexico. Since the river's runnin' real high and fast, I doubt they'll attempt to cross it, but if they do, they'll most likely get swept away and drowned. If they try leavin' by way of Presa Canyon, we'll be right on their butts before they get halfway up the switchback trail that leads outta there. There's no chance they can outrun us if they try that."

"And if they decide to double back?" Joe Driscoll, the youngest man in the patrol, said.

"Well, son, if they do that, we won't have any problem findin' 'em at all, will we?" Ben answered, before Luke had the chance. "Luke," he continued, "How're we gonna handle this bunch, especially since it appears there's about a dozen or more of them, and only seven of us?"

"Yeah, I know, Ben. It hardly seems fair to those hombres, us havin' 'em outnumbered like that."

"That's why you lose so much of the time at the gamblin' tables, Luke. You never can figure the odds right."

"Oh, I think I've got 'em down pretty good this time," Luke replied. "It ain't the number of men we're up against I'm worried about. It's the terrain. There's more'n a few places in there where those boys could hole up and pick us off. There's side canyons, cliffs, rockslides, large boulders, and plenty of scrub brush. There's also quite a few caves. We're gonna have to go into that canyon real careful, and stay alert every minute. I don't particularly feel like takin' a dry-gulcher's bullet in the back. Once we do catch up with that outfit, we'll have to spread out, and take cover ourselves. It's gonna be one helluva fight, chousin' those men outta that canyon. I don't want to make it even harder by ridin' into a trap."

"When we locate those men, are we gonna give 'em a chance to surrender?" Joe asked.

The other men in the patrol chuckled.

"Ah, the sweet innocence of youth," Ben muttered. "Son, if you keep thinkin' like that, you'll be dead before your next birthday. It's kill or be killed, kid. If you get one of those bastards in your sights, even if it's his back you're lookin' at, you put a bullet in him, before he gets the chance to put one in you, or one of your pardners. That outfit we're after is led by Matt Spencer. He's one of the meanest son of a bitches ever to walk the same earth as decent folks. Down in Laredo, he once killed a man just for bumpin' into him. Shot the poor *hombre* dead in the street, then gunned down the town marshal, and a deputy, who tried to arrest him. Made his getaway by crossin' the Rio into Mexico. He's a snake-eyed, cold blooded killer. Most of the men ridin' with him are almost as bad. You get the chance, don't even hesitate. Kill any of 'em you can."

"But we're the law," Joe objected. "We can't just shoot down someone without givin' him a chance to surrender, and have a fair trial, in front of a judge and jury."

"Joe, remind me again where you're from?" Luke said.

"Sure, Lieutenant. Texarkana, by way of Richmond, Virginia."

"So you were born back East, and your family moved to far northeast Texas?"

"That's right."

"And how long have you been a Ranger?"

11

"Just over a month."

"Let me explain somethin' to you, Joe, a bit more gently than the way Sergeant Thibodeaux is putting it. Things ain't as civilized out here as they are back East—for that matter, not even as civilized as in east Texas. Most places this far west, there's no law, except for us Rangers, and we're stretched way too thin. Even where there is a town, quite often it's too far away for us to haul prisoners, and it might not even have a jail. So, like it or not, if we're certain a man's guilty, sometimes we have to act as our own judge, jury, and even executioners. Mebbe that doesn't seem right, by your lights, but this is tough country, and we've gotta be as tough as the outlaws we're supposed to stop. That means we've got to fight them every bit as dirty as they fight us. Perhaps someday, if we, and the other lawmen out here, along with the decent folks attempting to settle up this territory, do our jobs right, it won't be that way, but for now, it is. Don't go feelin' sorry for the men we're after, neither. They're murderers, rustlers, and robbers. Every last man in that outfit is lookin' at the hang rope, or at the very least a long term behind bars. Not one of 'em is gonna give you a chance, so you can't give them one, either. If you do, they'll put a slug through you before you even knew what happened. I dunno if anyone's ever told you this, but the bullet you *don't* hear is the one that kills

12

you. The only warning they'll get is when I shout 'Texas Rangers!' So, if you don't understand that, and you're not willing to do the job that has to be done, say so right now. I'll accept your resignation, and you can ride away, with no hard feelings."

"No, Lieutenant. I'm a Texas Ranger, and I'm gonna do what I was hired on to do. I won't let you down."

"*Gracias*, Joe. I knew you had sand in your craw. One more thing. This is the Rangers, not the Army. We generally don't call each other by our ranks, unless we're at Headquarters, one of the big honchos, like Major Jones, is in camp, or when we're headin' into a fight. I'm Luke, and the sergeant is Ben. Understood?"

"Yessir, Lieutenant . . . I mean, Luke."

"Good. Everyone, listen up. We'll take a half hour to rest, and give the horses a breather. Use the time to check your weapons, eat a bit, or have a smoke. Soon as we ride out, there'll be no stoppin' for anything until we come up with that gang. Ben, I'll take the lead."

Ben laughed.

"I'm more'n willin' to let you take it, Luke, since that means you'll likely be shot at first. In which case, you'll take the *lead* and the *lead*."

"You always have been a joker, Ben," Luke retorted.

"Unless they let us get past 'em, and start

shootin' at us from behind," Zeb Prescott added. "In which case, I sure don't hanker to be the last man."

"I'll hang back," Ed Dunleavy said. "I'll try'n keep a lookout to our rear, best as I can."

"You've got it, Ed. I'm obliged," Luke said. "Besides, *your* rear's so skinny it makes a mighty poor target. That means you or your cousin Lonnie *should* bring up the rear. Any other questions?"

"Do you reckon those men know we're on their trail?" Shep Hawkins asked.

"Those men are outlaws, who've spent most of their adult lives runnin' from the law," Luke answered. "You can damn sure bet your hat they know we're after 'em."

"Which means they'll try and lead us right into a trap," Ben added.

"Ben's right, which also means we've got to outsmart those *hombres*, if any of us want to come out of that canyon alive," Luke said. "Any other questions?"

He got no response.

"Good. Thirty minutes."

Luke swung out of his saddle, loosened his cinches, and slid the bit out of Pete's mouth. Before tending to his own needs, he dug in his saddlebags for a leftover biscuit. He broke that in half, gave one piece to Pete, and the other to

Pete's brother, RePete, who was carrying a pack saddle. The two almost identically marked, sorrel and white paint geldings were a rarity, twin foals which had survived their mother's pregnancy, and were born healthy. In most cases, a mare in foal with twins usually either miscarried, or the babies were stillborn. Pete and RePete were lucky exceptions. Their original owner, as did many cowboys, had little use for paints, disdaining them as Indian ponies, or fancy mounts suitable only for women to ride. Luke had no such compunctions about riding a spotted horse. He recognized the potential in the pair of yearlings, and purchased them for a bargain price, saving them from being slaughtered for dog food. The now six-year-olds had justified his faith in them, growing up to be courageous under fire, with plenty of speed and stamina. More than once they had saved his life, either warning him of unseen danger, or outrunning his pursuers. After filling his hat from his canteen, and giving each horse a drink, he took some strips of jerky from his saddlebags, and chewed on those while the horses pulled at the sparse bunch grass.

Once Luke finished his meager meal, he washed down the dried meat with a swallow from his canteen, then rolled and lit a cigarette. He studied the men under his command while he smoked. First was Sergeant Ben Thibodeaux, his second in charge. The sergeant was a hardened veteran, a Cajun originally from Louisiana, bearded, dark featured, short and stocky, but lithe as a cat and tough as whang leather. Next was Ed Dunleavy, a long legged transplant from Tennessee, as were so many Texans. He was red-haired and green-eyed, with a smattering of freckles across his nose and cheeks. He was tenacious as a bulldog, never quitting, no matter how rough things might get. His cousin, Lonnie Montgomery, who had migrated to Texas with him, was also a redhead, but with blue eyes. He was as rugged as his cousin, and had the determination of a terrier locked onto a rat, when he was dealing with lawbreakers. Both were as tall and lanky as Thibodeaux was short and stocky. Luke sometimes wondered how they kept their gunbelts around their hips, rather than having them just slide down to their ankles. Zeb Prescott, sandy haired and gray eyed, was happy-go-lucky, always ready for a practical joke, so soft-spoken more than one man had underestimated him, until it was too late, and they found themselves behind bars . . . or six feet underground. Lastly, there were the two new men, Joe Driscoll and Shep Hawkins. Driscoll was only eighteen, with tow hair, pale blue eyes, and whiskers so light he appeared at least two years younger. Hawkins had just reached his nineteenth birthday a week ago. He had auburn hair which he wore shoulder length, hazel eyes, and a scar across his chin.

Neither had been tested under fire, so Luke wasn't certain how they would react when they faced their first gunfight.

Luke himself had been a Ranger for a little more than six years. He was thirty-two, just over six feet tall, and weighed a muscular one hundred and ninety pounds. He had an unusual combination of jet black hair and piercing blue eyes. He sported a meticulously groomed, thick moustache on his upper lip. His fair complexion had been darkened and toughened to the consistency of saddle leather by years of exposure to sun and wind. The black hair came from his part Choctaw, part French, part Scottish father, the blue eyes and fair skin from his Irish mother. His quick temper came from both. He wore a wide-brimmed, dirt- and sweat-stained brown Stetson, blue-checked shirt, a red bandanna looped around his neck, denims, and a leather vest. His brown boots were scuffed and well worn, the rowels of his spurs blunted, so as not to tear his horse's skin. A .45 caliber Colt Single Action Army pistol, better known as the Peacemaker, hung at his right hip, a long-bladed Bowie knife in a sheath on his left. A Model 1873 Winchester repeater rode in a saddle scabbard under his left leg. Since Texas Rangers wore no uniforms, nor did most carry badges, there was nothing to distinguish Luke, or any of the men riding with him, from any other chuck-line-riding cowboys or horse wranglers. However, snugged in his shirt pocket *was* a badge, a silver star in silver circle made from a Mexican *cinco peso* coin. While on assignment in the border town of Del Rio, he'd commissioned that badge from a Mexican silversmith.

Luke took a last drag on his quirly, tossed the butt to the dirt, and ground it out under his boot heel. He retightened his cinches, slid the bit back into Pete's mouth, then picked up his reins.

"Time to mount up, boys," he said, as he swung into his saddle.

Chapter 2

Seminole Canyon had been named for the Black Seminole Scouts, who were official recruits of the United States Army, many stationed at Fort Clark, Texas. A number of those men had served with distinction during campaigns against Apaches, Comanches, and Kiowas. Four would even become recipients of the Congressional Medal of Honor. The canyon also held several sites of pictographs, thousands-of-years-old rock paintings left by the original inhabitants of the area, who were now long vanished. Drained by Seminole Creek, the canyon wound mostly south for about a dozen miles, to where the creek emptied into the Rio Grande, several miles downstream from the mouth of the Pecos River. However, none of the history of Seminole Canyon, or its previous peoples, was on Luke's mind as he led his small band of Rangers into its depths. His only concern was finding the band of outlaws he and his men had been pursuing for nearly two weeks, and bringing their depredations to an end. Outnumbered by at least two to one, Luke knew he and his men would need to use every bit of fighting skill they had, as well as a lot of luck, to outwit their enemies.

If they succeeded, and lived, it would be because he had done his job right. If they didn't, then the blame would all be his.

Despite his years of being a Texas Ranger, and a town marshal before that, Luke always had a lump of fear, sitting like a chunk of ice in his belly, whenever he was heading into a gunfight. He'd been taught by his father, the long-time sheriff of Brazos County, that any man who felt no fear when facing another man's guns, was the one who would end up dead. It was good advice Luke had never forgotten.

Luke led his men slowly through the canyon, trying to make as little noise and raise as little dust as they could. While it was impossible to move silently through the dry brush on horseback, with the clopping of the horses' hooves, the jingle of bits, the squeaking of leather, and the animals' occasional snorts or nickers, there was no point in attracting unwanted attention by making more noise than necessary. Ben Thibodeaux pushed his lineback dun horse into a slightly faster walk, and rode up alongside Luke.

"It sure looks like those *hombres* are headed straight for the border," he said. "That's Presa Canyon we just passed."

"I know it," Luke answered. "I can't figure why they'd do that, with the Rio runnin' so high. They can't be so stupid they didn't realize it was in flood. They've got to know we're on their tails, and will have 'em backed against the river with no way out."

"Kinda caught between the devil and the deep blue sea, eh?" Ben said. He laughed. "I do have to wonder if they've got some plan, or another way out, we haven't figured on."

"It wouldn't surprise me one bit," Luke answered. "We'll know before long. It's only about four more miles to the Rio. Y'know, Ben, it's been quite some time since I've been in this canyon. It's wider and more open than I remember."

"Yeah, it is," Ben agreed. "It's not at all like some of those damn slot canyons, that'll give a man claus . . . claustro . . . Hell, what do they call it when a man gets to feelin' all closed in, can't hardly breathe, and starts to panic?"

"Claustrophobia."

"That's it. Anyway, this here place isn't like that at all."

Indeed, Seminole Canyon was fairly wide, especially for this region, and not as deep as many others. There was more of the sky visible from the canyon floor, and the walls didn't seem quite so tall and threatening.

"In one way that's good," Luke said. "It'll make it harder for those *hombres* to set up an ambush. But, it also gives them more places to hide, or hole up until we quit lookin' for 'em."

"It don't matter," Ben said, with a shrug. "Until

we find those sons of bitches, they've got all the advantage. We're liable not to know we've come up on 'em until the bullets start flyin'."

"Let's hope it doesn't come to that. I know one thing for certain. It's too doggone quiet in here. No birds flyin', no jackrabbits flushin' outta the bushes, not even many insects buzzin' around. That means somethin's disturbed all the critters, and driven 'em to ground. That can only be the men we're after. They mustn't be too far ahead of us now."

Ben fell back. He kept the rest of the men strung out behind him, so they wouldn't bunch up and make one easier target. They had ridden for another two miles, when Joe Driscoll put his horse into a trot, and rode up to Thibodeaux.

"Somethin' bothering you, Joe?" Ben asked.

"Yeah, Sarge. I think I just saw some movement up ahead, off to the right."

"Keep movin'." Ben ordered. "Don't point, but exactly where?"

"At the spot where the canyon curves left. There's a slide at that curve. Look about halfway up the slide, where there's a ridge of rocks, busted up trees, and rubble. I'm pretty certain I spotted some dust risin' from behind that ridge. Thought I caught just a glimpse of a man's head just as he ducked behind one of the rocks, too."

"Let's talk to the lieutenant."

Luke had heard Joe approaching, and slowed

his horse, waiting for the young Ranger and veteran sergeant to reach his side.

"What've you got, Ben?" he asked.

"Joe here's pretty certain he saw a puff of dust comin' from that slide up ahead, and a man hidin' behind the ridgeline halfway up the talus slope."

Luke chanced taking a quick look at the slide, knowing the brim of his Stetson would most likely conceal his movement.

"That's a jim-dandy place to set up an ambush, all right," he said. "Are you certain you saw somethin' up there, Joe?"

"Almost one hundred percent. I happened to see a couple of jaybirds flyin' out from the trees near the ridge, when I took off my hat to wipe some sweat outta my eyes. They were squawkin' and complainin'. That made me curious, so I kept watchin' to see what might've disturbed those fellers. That's when I saw the dust, then the man. Now, look close and you'll see there's a hawk soarin' away from the same spot. He's screamin' his head off, so he's sure enough mad about somethin' that disturbed him."

"You've got sharp eyes, Joe. Good work. We'll pull up at that clump of mesquite just ahead and figure out what our next move is."

"Won't those *hombres* get suspicious if we stop now?" Joe asked.

"If they're waitin' for us up where you claim you saw them, you can be certain they've already spotted us, so it won't make any difference," Luke answered.

"Besides, they probably think we have no idea we've found them, and realize they're up on that slide, just waitin' for us to ride into rifle range, so they can cut us down from ambush, the dirty backshooters," Ben added. "They'll more'n likely figure we're just takin' a break, and givin' the horses a breather. Let's keep goin'."

They rode the short distance to the mesquites, then under their branches, into the welcome shade. Luke told the men to remain in their saddles. Once those who wished had rolled and lit cigarettes, he explained their situation.

"All right, men, here's what we're up against. Joe claims he spotted an *hombre* ducking behind a ridgeline halfway up that landslide about a quarter mile away. If he's right, that means the men we're trailin' have stopped runnin', and have picked a damn good spot for a drygulchin'."

"How certain are you about that, Joe?" Zeb asked.

"Damn certain. I spotted some birds that were flushed from up there, then dust, and a man's head as he took cover behind the rocks. There was a hawk yellin' at something up on that slide, too."

"Whether Joe's seen somethin' or not doesn't really matter," Luke said. "That ridge is a right likely spot for an ambush, so we've got no choice but to assume Joe's right, and plan accordingly. The worst that can happen if Joe's wrong is we keep after those *hombres*. But if he's right, and I'm betting he is, we don't want to just ride into a trap."

"I'm sure hopin' you've got an idea how to keep us out of that ambushin', Lieutenant," Shep said.

"I've got a couple," Luke answered. "I'll speak my piece, then listen to you men. Mebbe one of you'll come up with a better idea.

"First, we could just turn around, and ride away, allowing those men to escape."

"You're not serious, are you, Lieutenant?" Lonnie asked.

"Just rein in there, Lonnie," Luke answered. "I said we *could* just turn tail and flee. I didn't say we *would*. That's not the way us Rangers operate. I doubt any of us would be able to hold up our heads if we did that. I know I damn for certain couldn't. We'd be branded as cowards for the rest of our lives. The only way we might try that is if actin' like we were runnin' away would lure those *hombres* into chasin' after us. I don't imagine they're quite that stupid, so that's out."

"Second, we could just ride like hell, and hope most of us got past those men, then try and get to 'em when they come outta the rocks. That's not likely to work, bein' as they've got good cover, and we'll be out in the open. I don't know about the rest of you, but I'm not hankerin' to commit suicide today. Which brings me to our third option. We'll mosey along at a walk, as if we don't suspect a thing, until just before we get in range of their guns. Then, we'll ride hell bent for leather, shootin' as we go. The chances we'd hit anyone are mighty slim, but at least we might keep those sons of bitches pinned down, until we get to the bottom of the slide. We'll leave our saddles there, get under cover pronto, then start makin' our way up that slide. Once we're off our horses, there's plenty of rocks and stuff we can use for cover. With luck, we'll be able to work our way up to where those *hombres* are holed up. We should be able to outgun 'em if we can get close enough. I'm not gonna try'n pull the wool over your eyes, though. The odds are stacked against us. It's likely at least some of us will take a bullet today. If any of you think you've got a better plan, now's the time to say so."

"What about a couple of us tryin' to circle around, and come up behind that bunch?" Ed suggested.

"That's not a bad idea, Ed," Luke answered. "Ben, what do you think?"

"I've been studyin' the layout of that slide while we've been sittin' here, Luke," Ben answered. "There's no possible way, at least that I can see, to snake our way around the back. Even climbin' those rocks as you're suggesting is mighty risky. A lot of the soil in that slide is bound to be loose. One wrong step, and a man might start an avalanche that would bring the whole shebang down on us."

"As long as it brought those *hombres* down with it," Joe said, with a rueful smile. "That'd finish our job."

"Yeah, but we'd all be dead, squashed flatter'n a June bug under a boot heel," Lonnie objected.

"Well, I suppose that could be a drawback," Zeb conceded. "Just a minor one."

"Luke, the longer we sit here palaverin', the more likely it is those men will get suspicious they've been seen," Ben said. "Unless someone else has any better ideas, I'd suggest we get movin'."

"You're right. Fill your pockets with shells, men. Time to move out. Remember, keep your horses at an easy walk, until I put Pete into a gallop. Then, get low in your saddles, yell and scream like banshees, and ride like ol' Beelzebub himself was after you. Good luck, and may the Good Lord ride with us."

Even though he knew they were still out of range of the hidden outlaws' guns, Luke's stomach churned as he and his men drew nearer the landslide. If the gang had hidden a man somewhere closer to the trail, or waiting until the Rangers passed, he'd feel the searing pain of hot lead tearing through his back or guts before he got anywhere near his quarry. He forced himself to hold Pete, with RePete following close behind, to a walk, until he got as near to the slide as he dared, before digging his spurs into the paint's sides. The startled horse leapt forward in a dead run. Dropping the reins over his saddle horn, guiding Pete with only his knees, Luke yanked his Winchester from its scabbard, leaned low over his horse's neck, and sent several bullets in the general direction of the outlaws. For the moment, Luke's plan was working. Taken by surprise when the Rangers broke into a gallop, the outlaws' first shots came after Luke and his men reached the base of the slide, dove off their horses, and rolled into cover. The ambushers' first bullets either missed their targets completely, or ricocheted harmlessly away. Luke noted with satisfaction all of his comrades had safely made shelter, and were already starting their way up the jagged, rock and gravel strewn surface of the slide.

"Spread out!" Luke called to his men. "Stay under cover, as best you can. Try not to waste any shots!"

One of the outlaws poked his rifle over a fallen tree, aiming at Luke. Before he could pull the trigger, Luke took a hasty bead on the man's head and fired. His bullet punched through the man's forehead, exiting the back of his skull in a spray of blood and brain matter. The man's hat flew off, and he dropped out of sight.

"You men up in the rocks!" Luke yelled. "Matt Spencer! This is the Texas Rangers. You're under arrest, the whole bunch of you. Throw your weapons over the rocks and come out with your hands in the air!"

There was a moment of silence, then a mocking laugh.

"You're a real funny man, you know that, Ranger? I don't know how y'all figured out we were up here waitin' on you, but there's fifteen of us, and only seven of you. We've got you outnumbered, and the high ground besides. The only chance any of you bastards have of leavin' here alive today is if you make a run for your horses, and hope and pray you can reach them and ride away before we put bullets in your backs."

"There's only fourteen of you," Luke shouted back. "I've already put a bullet through one man's brain."

"That was Petey. He didn't have no brains anyhow."

Before Luke could respond, a shot rang out to his left. Another outlaw screeched in pain, grabbed his stomach, jackknifed, toppled over the rocks and slid halfway down the slope, his path marked by a thin trail of dust.

"That's two of you down now, you sons of

Satan!" Ben shouted. "That means thirteen left. Unlucky thirteen, you sons of bitches!"

He grinned at Luke, then scrambled across an open stretch of dirt. A bullet nipped at his heels as he slid behind a large cluster of prickly pear. Several more tore holes in the cactus's pads, or shot them off. Ben rolled to the more secure shelter of a precariously perched boulder, and took another shot, driving an outlaw back from the ridgeline.

The canyon erupted with the sound of gunfire and the smell of powder smoke, as the Rangers fought their way up the slope, determined to reach the outlaws they'd been trailing for so long. The outlaws, for their part, battled back desperately, knowing their capture would mean, for most if not all of them, a trip to the gallows.

Luke could only hope none of his men had been hit, having to focus solely on keeping himself safe, as he zigzagged his way up the slide. He shot one man, who was foolish enough to stand up to take a shot at him, through the chest, then drilled another one through his belly, sending him tumbling off the ridge. A searing flame tore through Luke's right leg, dropping him to one knee when a bullet punctured his thigh. His return shot missed the man who'd gotten him. The man fired again, his bullet striking Luke low in his gut. Luke fell to his side, rolled over, and put a slug through the outlaw's ribs. He forced himself to his feet, and, hunched over, resumed climbing, limping badly, struggling against the pain, fighting for breath. He caught a glimpse of Joe Driscoll when he shot one man out of a pin oak, then the youngster screamed in pain, clutched his chest, and pitched to his face. Off to Luke's left, Ben Thibodeaux shot another man, then was driven backwards by a bullet through his lungs. Luke knew, from the way Ben hit the ground and lay unmoving, the sergeant was either already dead, or nearly so.

"Dammit!" Luke cursed. "They're cuttin' us down, one man at a time. Well, they ain't gonna take me without a few more comin' along for the ride."

He summoned the last of his strength, lunged for the ridgeline, firing until his rifle was empty. He tossed the Winchester aside and pulled out his six-gun. He made the low wall of rocks and debris, and jumped over it. He was surprised to see the rest of his men, except for Ben and Joe, had already breached the outlaws' defenses, and were fighting fierce, man-to-man battles. One man came rushing toward Luke, brandishing a knife. Luke's quick shot, intended for the man's chest, instead struck the knife, knocking it out of his hand. The man's momentum carried him up to Luke, who shoved the barrel of his Peacemaker into the man's belly, thumbed back the hammer, and pulled the trigger. The outlaw took three more steps, then crumpled.

The gunfire was thinning out, as more men fell. Ed Dunleavy screamed, then sat down hard, and yelped again. Shep Hawkins killed the man who'd shot Ed, with a bullet in the back, then turned to face another oncoming gunman. He and the outlaw pulled their triggers at the same time. Both men went down, each shot in the stomach.

One of the last remaining outlaws popped up from where he'd taken cover, and drew a bead on Luke's back. Ed, from where he was sitting, put two bullets through the man's belly, just as he fired, spoiling his aim. The bullet he'd intended for Luke's spine instead tore through his upper right arm, nicking the bone and fracturing it. Luke dropped his gun, grabbed the wounded arm with his left hand, and fell to the dirt. The man who'd shot him was lying curled up on the ground, moaning, with his hands clamped to his bullet-torn belly.

After a final flurry of gunshots, silence descended on Seminole Canyon. Zeb Prescott hurried up to Luke.

"Lieutenant, how bad are you hit?" he asked.

"Pretty bad, but I should . . . be okay . . . Zeb. Give me a . . . hand up, will . . . you?"

"Shouldn't you just stay right where you're at, until we can patch you up?"

"No. Not until I check . . . on the other men."

"All right, but I still don't think it's a good idea."

Zeb pulled Luke to his feet, just as Lonnie Montgomery came over.

"Seems like we took a pretty good whippin', but we gave those bastards more'n what for," he said. "Only a couple of 'em are still breathin', and they won't be for long. Looks like you took a couple of slugs, Luke. Appears like one of 'em got you in the guts. You'd best lie down so we can see how bad it is."

"Don't worry about me right now. We've got to see to the others. I'm almost certain Ben Thibodeaux's dead. Same with Shep Hawkins. Joe Driscoll got hard hit, too. Lonnie, you'd better check on your cousin. He got shot, but he still managed to put a couple of slugs into the son of a bitch who shot me in the arm. He probably saved my life."

"I'm not hurt all that bad," Ed called, from where he was now lying on his stomach. The back of his whipcord trousers was soaked with blood. "One of those bastards got me in my butt. Once the bullet's dug out, I'll be fine. Of course, it's gonna be kinda hard sittin' down, for quite a spell."

"Not to mention settin' a horse," Lonnie said, with a grim smile.

"Ed, how in the world did you catch a bullet in your butt, skinny as your rear is?" Zeb asked.

"I reckon it was just my bad luck. You and Lonnie go with Luke, to see about the other boys. My hurts can wait."

"Lonnie, you go check on Shep, then after that see to your cousin," Luke ordered. "Zeb, you come with me. We'll look at Ben, then Joe."

Ben Thibodeaux was indeed already dead. Incongruously, the tough old veteran had a wide grin frozen on his face.

"Gee, that's pretty strange," Zeb said. "The sarge looks like he died happy."

"I'm sure he did," Luke said. "The Rangers were his entire life. He always said he wanted to go out fightin'. He got his wish. Plus he downed a couple of men before they got him. He probably died laughin' and cussin' at 'em. Let's see about Joe."

"You're still bleedin' bad, Luke," Zeb said. "Why don't you wait here while I check on him?"

"Uh-uh." Luke shook his head. "Not a chance. If Joe's still alive, but mortally hit, I want to talk to him, tell him what a good job he did, before he cashes in his chips. After that, I'll listen to you. But I've got to be certain about Joe."

"All right."

Zeb helped Luke over to where Joe still lay where he had fallen, face down in the rocks.

"Will you be able to stand while I roll this poor kid over, Luke?" Zeb asked.

"Yeah. I'm gettin' a mite weak, but I'll manage."

"All right."

Zeb carefully rolled Joe onto his back.

"Luke, Joe's still breathin'," he said. "He's hurt pretty bad, though. He took a slug in his chest. I can't tell for certain if it hit a lung or not. I don't believe it did. The bullet hit pretty high up, on the left side, and I don't see any froth around his lips, or blood bubblin' from his mouth or nose. His breathing's strong and regular, too. Since there's no exit wound in his back, the bullet must still be in him."

"That's good news. At least he ain't dead," Luke said. He hobbled over to stand alongside the wounded young Ranger.

"Joe, can you hear me?" he asked. "It's Luke. Lieutenant Caldwell."

Joe's eyes flickered open.

"Lieutenant?" He tried to sit up, but fell back.

"Take it easy, son. You took a bullet in your chest. Zeb's here with me. We'll get you patched up. You're gonna be all right."

"Damn. It hurts somethin' awful," Joe said. "Like someone stuck a hot poker in me, and is movin' it all around inside my chest. It sure as hell doesn't *feel* like I'm gonna pull through."

"Once we get that bullet out it won't hurt quite as bad, son."

"How about the rest of the boys?"

"Ben's dead, and Shep probably is. Ed and you are wounded, Ed not too badly. He'll be fine."

"The renegades?"

"All dead, or dyin'."

"Don't forget to tell the kid you got shot up pretty good, too, Luke," Zeb said.

Luke gave him an exasperated look.

"Zeb . . . Never mind, it's too late, since you just spilled the beans."

"You thought you'd be able to keep that from him?" Zeb retorted.

"No, I reckon not," Luke admitted.

"You . . . you're hurt too, Luke? How bad?" Joe asked.

"Just a couple of scrapes. I'll be fine."

"Lieutenant?"

"What, Joe?"

"I reckon my eyes . . . ain't as good as you said."

"How's that, son?"

"I never saw the bullet comin'. Never even saw the *hombre* who pulled the trigger."

He managed a soft laugh.

"You usually don't see the one that gets you, Joe," Luke answered, with a laugh of his own. "Besides, you blasted at least one of those *hombres* out of a tree and straight to Hell. You did good, son. Real good. Unless I miss my guess, you're gonna be a man to ride the river with. You can bet your hat on it."

"Thanks. Thanks, Luke. But I'd have to find my hat, first. Dunno what happened to it."

Joe laughed, then drifted back into unconsciousness.

"Zeb?"

"Yeah, Luke?"

"Better hold me up."

Luke's knees buckled. Zeb grabbed him under the armpits before he collapsed. He lowered him to the ground.

"You'd best let me see how bad those wounds are, and I mean right now, Luke," he said. "Joe's will have to wait until I care for you."

"Reckon mebbe . . . I'd better," Luke conceded.

Zeb opened Luke's shirt, to first check the belly wound.

"This slug got you down low. Real low, Luke," Zeb noted. "The wound's still oozing blood. It looks like the slug's still somewhere in your guts. I can't tell if it hit any of your vitals, but it damn for certain ain't good."

"Bein' gutshot usually isn't," Luke answered. He managed a soft chuckle.

"Tell me somethin' I don't already know," Zeb said. He pulled the bandanna from around his neck, folded it, and placed it over the bullet hole. After tearing a strip from the bottom of his shirt to tie the bandage in place, he then took out his knife, and cut open the seams of Luke's pants leg. There were two holes in Luke's thigh, one in back, another larger one, in front.

"Well, I've got *some* good news for you, at

37

least," he said. "This slug went clean through your leg. It missed the bone. Once I stop the bleedin', we won't have to worry about this one, until later. I'll need your neckerchief."

He removed the cloth from Luke's neck, and tied it around his leg.

"Now, lemme take a look at that arm."

When Zeb attempted to roll up Luke's sleeve, Luke screamed in agony.

"Damn it, Zeb, what the hell are you tryin' to do, rip my arm off?" he said, through teeth gritted against the pain.

"I barely got started, Luke," Zeb answered. "That ain't good. I reckon your arm's busted."

Instead of rolling the sleeve up, Zeb cut it off at the shoulder.

"The arm's sure enough broke," he said. "I'll have to splint it."

Zeb peeled off his own shirt, and tore a strip from it to wrap around the hole in Luke's arm.

"Don't move, Luke. You don't want to chance shiftin' the bone and makin' the break worse. I've got to find a pair of straight branches for a splint."

"You'd better plug the hole in Joe's chest first, before he bleeds out," Luke answered. "I promise I won't go anywhere."

"I don't imagine you will," Zeb answered. "It's a deal."

Zeb turned his attention back to Joe, who had

regained consciousness, but had remained silent while Zeb worked on Luke.

"Kid, you're awake," Zeb said. "That's a good sign. I'm gonna plug the hole in you, just to stop the bleedin' for now. Once that's done, I've got to splint Luke's arm. It's busted. Soon as that's fixed, I'll come back to you. Okay?"

"Sure, it's okay, Zeb," Joe answered.

"Good. Let me get at it."

Zeb unbuttoned Joe's shirt, revealing a bullet hole high on the left side of his chest, just beneath the shoulder blade.

"You're still bleedin', but not too badly," Zeb told him. "Luckily, it appears that the bullet missed your lung, or you'd be meetin' your Maker pretty darn quick. I'm gonna have to use your shirt for a bandage. Soon as I'm done settin' Luke's arm, I'll try to dig the bullet outta you."

"Just make certain the lieutenant's taken care of," Joe said. "Don't worry about me."

"That's enough of that kinda talk," Zeb snapped. "I'll take care of both of you. Now hold still while I patch you up."

It only took a few moments for Zeb to get the bandage in place around Joe's chest. He was just finishing up when Lonnie walked over.

"How's Joe and the lieutenant doin', Zeb?" he asked.

"I just finished with Joe here, at least for now. Luke's in worse shape. He took a bullet in his gut, another through his leg, and one that busted his arm. I've stopped his bleeding, as well as Joe's, the best I can. I'm going to cut down a couple of saplings or branches to splint the arm. How's Ed? And what about Shep?"

"Shep bled out just as I got to him. He didn't say a word before he took his last breath. Hard as this sounds, it's better that he died quick, rather'n lingerin'. Ed should be all right, once the bullet's pulled out of his rump. He won't be settin' a horse anytime soon, though, I wouldn't think."

"If you two could quit jabberin' like magpies, even if only for a couple of minutes, I've got somethin' to say, before I pass out," Luke spoke up. "One of you get Ed over here."

"Sure," Lonnie said. "I'll bring him right back."

"Are you gettin' weaker, Luke?" Zeb asked, while Lonnie went for Ed.

"Yeah, Zeb. Kinda light headed."

"Mebbe I should start tryin' to find that slug in your gut right now."

"No. Don't. Just hold on until I say what I've gotta say. Wait until Ed and Lonnie are both here."

"Okay, but I'm not certain waitin' is a good idea."

It only took a moment for Lonnie to return with Ed, who was limping heavily, but walking without any help.

"We're both here, Luke," Lonnie said.

"Good. Got a question for you, Ed. Can you ride?"

"It'll hurt like hell, but yeah, I believe so," Ed answered. "If you need me to, I'll manage."

"Good. Then we're headin' back to camp."

"Hold on just one doggone minute there, Luke," Zeb said. "You're not sayin' we're ridin' outta here, are you?"

"That's exactly what I'm sayin'. Soon as you get the horses rounded up, then Ben and Shep's bodies wrapped in their blankets and tied over their saddles, we're movin' out."

"Forgive my sayin' so, Lieutenant, but have you gone plumb loco?" Lonnie exclaimed. "You're in no shape to go anywhere. Neither is Joe. Ed isn't either, when you come right down to it."

"We've got no choice. If we stay here, I'll either bleed to death, or die of blood poisoning from the bullet in my belly. We're less than twenty miles from D's main camp. There's an almost full moon tonight, so it'll be light enough to see to travel. If we keep a steady pace, we should arrive at camp by sunup, mebbe even a bit earlier. Once we're there, Doc Mathis can tend to our hurts."

"Luke, or I guess I'd better say Lieutenant, with all due respect, that's the most damn foolish idea I've ever heard," Zeb said. "We can't risk movin' you or Joe, and perhaps having one of those bullets you're both carryin' moving inside

41

you, and finishin' you off. Hell, even the motion of your horse might start either one of you to bleedin' again. Besides, you yourself said you were just about ready to pass out."

"I'm feelin' better. Good enough to straddle my horse and ride, at least."

"Have I got a say in this?" Joe asked.

"I reckon you do," Luke answered.

"Then I say we follow the lieutenant's advice, Zeb. He's been a Ranger longer'n any of the rest of us. I'd imagine he knows what he's talkin' about."

"You don't understand exactly how bad off you are, kid," Zeb answered. "You twist wrong, and the bullet in your chest moves, just the tiniest fraction of an inch, it could punch a hole in your lung and kill you."

"So could doin' nothin'."

"That's why I plan on pulling the slugs out of you and the lieutenant before we try to head for camp," Zeb said.

"All of you, listen to me," Luke said. "Until I'm dead, or no longer capable of making decisions, I'm still in charge of this patrol. Ed, have you ever dug a bullet out of a man?"

"No, I can't say as I have, Luke."

"Lonnie?"

Lonnie blushed, and shook his head.

"No, Luke, I'm afraid I haven't either," he admitted.

"Well, I damn sure have, more'n a few times," Zeb said, angrily.

"I know you have, Zeb," Luke answered. "But you've only done it when you had someone else, with more experience, guiding you. You've also only removed bullets from a man's arm or leg, mebbe his ribs, or a hip. But, as far as I know, you've never poked around inside a man's belly, or a man's chest, to try and find a slug buried deep inside someone. It's one thing to work on a man when you're not near his vitals. It's a whole 'nother can of worms to search for a bullet inside a man's guts, or right next to his lungs, heart, or maybe his spine. In the first instance, you're not liable to kill a man if your hand slips, or you probe a little too deep. In the second, one slight mistake could kill or paralyze the *hombre* you're workin' on. I won't put that burden on you. Perhaps if we weren't so near camp, then I would, because there'd be no other choice. Since we are, what we're gonna do is this. Lonnie, you ride ahead, as fast as you can. Let Captain Garrison know what's happened. Let him know he'll need to send some men out here to pick up what's left of the Spencer gang. They'll want to bring back those *hombres'* horses and gear, too. We can use those. Make Doc Mathis aware he'll have some surgery to perform. Zeb, you and Ed'll get me and Joe back to camp. We'll take Ben and Shep with us. That way, they can have a decent

43

burial, with some words said over 'em. Lonnie, get started."

"Sure thing, Luke. I'll have Cap'n Shaver send some men out to meet you. Take care."

"*Bueno*. We'll see you in camp."

Lonnie went to retrieve his bay, then start the ride to camp.

"Zeb, you and Ed'll have to help me on my horse," Luke said. "Joe on his, too."

"Lieutenant, if you're that worried about the slug you took movin' around inside your belly, you shouldn't be ridin' at all. We'll make a travois for you, and another one for Joe."

"No, that'd take too much time," Luke said. "All you need to do is replace our bandages, then get us in our saddles. I'll tie myself to Pete's back. You can rope Joe to his horse."

"I'll say it again. What about you bein' light-headed?" Zeb insisted.

"And I'll say it again. I'm feelin' a lot better, now that the bleeding seems to have stopped. However, I am gonna tie myself to my horse, in case I do pass out. Don't worry. If I should start bleedin' heavy again, I'll let you know. In that case, we'll stop, and you won't have any choice other than to try'n dig the bullet outta me. Joe, the same goes for you. If you start bleedin' real bad, you let Zeb or Ed know, pronto."

"Okay, Luke."

"Zeb, I'll get the horses and load up Ben and

Shep, while you finish up with Luke and Joe," Ed said.

"All right."

Within half an hour, Ben's and Shep's bodies were loaded belly down over their saddles, Luke and Joe were tied to their horses' backs, while Jeb and Ed were mounted, each leading a horse carrying one of their dead comrades.

"Make the best time you can, Zeb, but don't push the horses into anything more than a slow jog," Luke ordered. "At that pace, we should make camp about an hour before first light."

"Okay, Luke. C'mon, Pegasus, let's go."

Zeb heeled his white gelding into a smooth walk.

Luke became unconscious before an hour passed. He spent almost the entire ride drifting in and out of that state, fighting to remain upright in the saddle, but most of the time riding slumped over his horse's neck. Several hours later, he did jerk upright at the sound of a group of rapidly approaching riders.

"Someone's comin', Zeb."

"I heard 'em, Luke," Zeb answered. "They don't seem to be tryin' to keep from bein' discovered. We're not all that far from camp. It's probably Lonnie, leading some of the men to meet us. Here they come now."

Several men came around a bend in the trail.

In the lead was Lonnie, with Sergeant Sean O'Malley alongside him. Zeb called to them.

"Lonnie. Sergeant. Over here!"

The other Rangers, five in all, trotted their horses up, then reined to a halt.

"Howdy, Zeb," Lonnie said. "You made better time than we expected. You're only about three miles from camp. How's Luke and Joe doin'? And you, Ed?"

"Not very good, I'm afraid. They're both still alive, but just barely. Joe's been unconscious the entire way, while Luke keeps fadin' in and out. He's been saggin' in his saddle since we started out."

"Far as me, my rump hurts something fierce, but I'll be okay," Ed added.

"I'm . . . fine . . ." Luke tried to say, but passed out once again.

"You'd better hurry and get those two to camp, if they're to have any chance at all," O'Malley said. "Doc Mathis is waitin' for 'em."

"*Bueno*. We'll see you back in camp," Zeb said. He spurred Pegasus into a slow jogtrot.

Private Sam Bartles was on sentry duty at the entrance to Company D's campsite. He waved to Zeb to pull up, for just a moment.

"Doc Mathis is waitin' at his tent for you, Zeb," he said. "Captain Shaver is with him. Head straight on over there."

"All right."

Doctor Walter Mathis, a former field doctor for the Confederate Army, was Company D's surgeon. Unlike so many former military physicians, who had been cashiered out of the service for drunkenness or incompetence, Mathis was an expert surgeon, especially skilled at caring for gunshot wounds. He was also a teetotaler. In his early sixties, with salt and pepper hair, a spade beard, and piercing blue eyes behind thick pince-nez spectacles, Mathis exuded confidence, with his brusque, no nonsense manner. He, along with Captain Hal Shaver and two other Rangers, was standing outside his tent.

"How bad are those two?" he asked, once Zeb reached him.

"Real bad," Zeb answered. "Joe's in rough shape, but Luke's even worse off. He's feverish, and been delirious for the last two miles. Keeps screamin' about bein' surrounded by Comanches, then callin' out for his wife and kids."

"Bring them inside, and I'll get to work on them," Mathis ordered.

"You heard the doc, men," Shaver said. "Get 'em down."

Luke and Joe were untied from their saddles, lifted from their horses, and carried inside Mathis's tent. They were placed on the two sturdy tables he used for surgery.

"Larry, I want you to stay here as my assistant,

since you've worked with me before," Mathis ordered Larry Maloney, one of the veteran Rangers. "The rest of you get outside. As soon as I have anything to tell you, I'll let you know."

"There's nothing we can do but wait, boys," Garrison said. "Let's get outta Doc's way."

Mathis first made a cursory examination of Joe's wound, and immediately decided he was in more stable condition than Luke.

"Larry, Ranger Driscoll's going have to wait until I try and save Lieutenant Caldwell," he said. "Driscoll's got a halfway decent chance, but it will be a miracle if I can pull Caldwell through, with that belly wound. I'm amazed he's lasted this long. Hand me the chloroform, please."

"Sure, Doc."

Maloney took a brown bottle off a shelf, uncorked it, and handed it to Mathis, who took it, then bent low over Luke, whose eyes had flickered open.

"Luke. Lieutenant Caldwell. This is Doctor Mathis. You're back in camp. Can you hear me?"

Luke mumbled something unintelligible.

"I'll take that as a yes," Mathis said. "I'm ready to start operating on you. That bullet in your abdomen has got to come out, right now. It's been in there far too long. I'm about to give you a dose of chloroform to put you to sleep. Do you understand?"

Luke managed a slight nod of his head.

"Good. I'll get started."

Mathis poured a small amount of chloroform onto a folded cloth, then held that over Luke's mouth and nose, until he fell asleep.

Three hours later, Mathis emerged from his tent, wiping his hands on a bloodied cloth. Captain Shaver, Zeb Prescott, and Ed Dunleavy were waiting for him.

"How are Joe and Luke, Doc?" Shaver asked.

Mathis arched his back to remove a kink before answering.

"Ranger Driscoll should be fine, after a while, unless he develops an infection. I pulled the bullet out of his chest without much of a problem. Most of the damage was to the muscle, so the wound should heal relatively quickly, and without permanent damage."

"And Luke?"

Mathis shook his head.

"I just can't say. He should have already been dead, well before he reached camp. I dug the bullet out of his abdomen, sewed together several holes it had punctured through his intestines, and sterilized the wound. He's got a fever, which means infection is already setting in. He's liable to develop peritonitis from the bowel material which spilled out of the holes in his guts. If he does, he will have virtually no chance of survival. In addition, I had to clean and pack the wound in his leg, and bandage that. I also cleaned, dressed, and splinted his broken arm. All I can do for him now is try to keep the fever down, and hope the infection doesn't turn into blood poisoning. Right now, both he and Ranger Driscoll are resting, as comfortably as they can be. Larry is watching them for now."

"What you're sayin' is Luke doesn't stand a snowball's chance in Hell of living more'n a couple of days," Shaver said.

Mathis shrugged.

"I'm not certain. Ordinarily, I'd say your assessment is correct, Captain. However, there is a Doctor George Goodfellow, over in Arizona, who is establishing quite a reputation for his treatment of gunshot wounds to the abdomen. I've read several of his papers, and I used his procedures on Lieutenant Caldwell. Many of his theories particularly emphasize cleanliness, washing the hands and sterilizing the instruments carefully, to prevent contaminating the wound. I followed his recommendations while working on the lieutenant. That may slightly improve his chances. However, there are two major caveats. Doctor Goodfellow is especially clear, that a man who is gutshot *must* be operated on within an hour of obtaining his wound, to have any realistic chance of survival. Otherwise, the victim inevitably succumbs to internal hemorrhaging. Obviously, it has been far more than an hour since Lieutenant Caldwell was shot. While Ranger Prescott did an admirable job of slowing the bleeding, at least the external bleeding, nevertheless, the lieutenant has lost a considerable amount of blood. Also, the length of time which passed from the time Lieutenant Caldwell was shot until I was able to remove the bullet greatly increases the risk of infection. However, where there is life, there is always hope. All I can do now is monitor Lieutenant Caldwell, keep his fever from rising too high, and hope the infection runs its course. I must say his chances of surviving are still no more than twenty per cent, probably less. I'll also be monitoring Ranger Driscoll, of course."

"Is there anything we can do to help, Doc?" Shaver asked.

"I'll need someone to remain with my patients while I get some rest," Mathis answered. "That, and prayers. Those might be the most important medicine right now. Lieutenant Caldwell's recovery is out of my hands, and in God's. Ranger Dunleavy, I'm ready to remove the bullet from your buttocks now."

"Doc, you look awful tired," Ed answered. "I can wait while you get some shut-eye. I'll just lie on my belly until you wake up. Havin' this slug in my rump a few more hours won't make any difference."

"No, you're wrong, son," Mathis answered.

"I'm concerned I may already have left your wound go untreated too long as it is, Ranger; however, I had no choice but to operate on Lieutenant Caldwell and Ranger Driscoll first, due to the severity of their wounds. And believe me, once the bullet is removed, you'll have plenty of time to lie on your belly while you recuperate. If you'll kindly step inside my tent, remove your britches and drawers, then lie down on the table, I'll begin to work on you immediately."

"That sounds rather 'cheeky,' Doc," Zeb said, laughing.

"That warn't funny, Zeb," Ed snapped.

"I'm sorry, Ed. I really am. But I just couldn't resist making a 'crack' like that."

Zeb laughed even harder. Ed glowered at him.

"Zeb, go tend to the horses, or get some rest, or something, anything. Just get the hell out of here," Shaver ordered. "And Ed, get your butt in Doc's tent, so he can get the lead out of it!"

"Both of you?" Ed answered, grumbling. "All right, all right. I'm goin', before those damn jokes make me feel worse'n the bullet I took. C'mon, Doc, let's get this over with."

Chapter 3

For ten days Luke clung to life, the fever raging while his body fought the infection ravaging his system. Finally, early in the morning of the eleventh day, the crisis came, and passed. Luke's fever spiked, then gradually dropped. By early afternoon it was practically gone. Shortly before suppertime, he awakened. The canvas roof above him seemed vaguely familiar, as did the mingled scents of medicines, soaps, and chemicals. He could feel the pressure of the splint binding his arm, the bandages wrapped around his leg and belly, and the sheet covering him to his waist.

"Where . . . where am I?" he murmured, his voice weak and hoarse.

Larry Maloney, who was keeping watch over Luke and Joe, had dozed off in his chair. He stirred when he heard Luke speak.

"Lieutenant. You're awake, thank God," he said. "You're back in camp, in Doc Mathis's tent. He just went to have his supper. Hold on while I fetch him. I'll be right back."

Luke passed out again. He was reawakened by Doctor Mathis calling his name, and shaking his shoulder.

"Luke. Lieutenant Caldwell. It's Doctor Mathis. I'm sure glad to see you coming around.

We nearly lost you. It's been touch and go ever since you got back. I know this is going to sound like a stupid question, but how are you feeling?"

"Awfully weak, Doc. Kinda like a washed-out dishrag. I'm real thirsty, too."

"Both are to be expected," Mathis reassured him. "What about pain?"

"Yeah. I've got a headache, my belly's sore, and I feel pretty achy all over."

"Again, all that is to be expected. What about your arm and leg?"

"They don't feel too awful bad, just sort of stiff."

"Excellent. Do you have any sharp, stabbing pains anywhere, particularly in your abdomen?"

"You mean my gut, Doc? No, just a dull ache."

"Any sensations of tingling, prickling, or excessive heat, particularly in the area of your wounds?"

"Not really. In fact, I'm feeling nice and cozy, or so it seems."

"I know this will be hard for you to realize, until you're a bit stronger, but now that you've awakened, you should recover from your wounds rather quickly, since you'll be able to take nourishment and fluids. Up until now, between the infection and fever, your progress has been quite slow."

Luke suddenly remembered the wounded Joe Driscoll.

"Joe! How's Joe?" he exclaimed.

"Ranger Driscoll? He's doing just fine, and will make a full recovery. The bullet which struck him didn't hit any vital organs, nor did it damage any bones or ligaments. It lodged in the muscle. Extracting it from his chest was a relatively easy procedure. He did develop a minor fever, but that cleared up in less than three days. He's in the cot right alongside you. I gave him some laudanum to help him sleep. You'll be able to speak with him tomorrow."

"That's great news," Luke said. "How about Ed Dunleavy?"

"He won't be riding a horse for a few weeks, but he'll be fine, except for the scar, of course," Mathis answered.

"That scar won't bother Ed none," Larry said, with a laugh. "He'll show it off when he's in town and visits the sportin' gals. He'll either make up some yarn about how he got it fightin' off a horde of wild Comanches single-handed, savin' all his pards from a plumb awful death, or else he'll work up the gals' sympathy with a sad story about how much it still hurts, and the only thing that makes the pain go away is the tender touch of a female's fingertips. Hell, if he gets drunk enough, he might even drop his britches right in the middle of a saloon and let everyone have a look at it."

"Enough," Mathis ordered, brusquely. "Lieu-

55

tenant, I need to check your heart, pulse, and abdomen."

"Sure. But first, how long have I been out? And exactly how bad off am I, Doc?" Luke asked.

"You've been unconscious for nearly eleven days," Mathis answered. "Your condition when you arrived was very grave. You have a broken humerus from a bullet wound in your right arm, and a bullet passed cleanly through your right thigh. While those are both fairly serious injuries, they are not, normally, life-threatening. However, the wound to your lower abdomen is one that most men would not have survived. Besides the loss of blood, the bullet caused several puncture wounds to your intestines, which required extensive suturing. Bowel material which leaked out of those holes led to a severe infection, despite my best efforts to sterilize the injuries. By any reasonable medical standard, you should have died before you even made it as far as this camp, or succumbed shortly thereafter from extreme internal hemorrhaging and blood poisoning. I'm convinced only two things led to your survival. One is the procedures for treating abdominal wounds being pioneered by a Doctor George Goodfellow. I've been reading up on his methods, which are truly pioneering, and will be a great advance in the field of abdominal surgery for gunshot or stab wounds. The second is the intervention of God Almighty. He had to have kept you alive long enough for me to operate, and guided my hands while I did. In fact, He deserves far more credit than I do."

"I can't argue with you there, Doc. Of course, the Good Lord probably figured I was too ornery for Him to want me, at least yet."

"There is one other person who was instrumental in your remaining alive until you could reach the medical help you needed," Mathis continued. "Zeb Prescott did an exemplary job of field dressing your wounds, especially in slowing the abdominal bleeding. His excellent work prevented you from bleeding to death before you arrived here in camp. He also quite possibly saved Joe Driscoll's life. That's enough talking for now. It's important you don't overextend yourself. Once I check you over, Lieutenant, I'll allow you to have some weak broth, if you're able to keep it down. After that, I'll give you some laudanum to help you sleep. I know you won't want to believe me, but at this point, you need rest, more than anything else. It's nature's best medicine."

Mathis used his stethoscope to listen to Luke's heart, lungs, and abdomen.

"So far, so good, Lieutenant," he said. "Your lungs are clear, your heartbeat is strong and steady, and your bowel sounds are normal, although we'll have to wait until you're able to eat solid food, before we'll know for certain your belly wound has completely healed. I'm going to take your pulse now."

Mathis took Luke's left wrist to check his pulse rate.

"Excellent. Your heart rate is sixty four beats per minute. That's quite good. Just one more thing, then I'll be done for now. I want to see if you still have a fever."

Mathis placed his hand on Luke's forehead, and held it there for a moment.

"You're doing even better than I expected, Lieutenant," he said. "Your fever is completely gone. That means your body has fought off the infection. Larry, please go ask Jonesy to heat up some beef broth for the lieutenant. While you do that, I'll clean his wounds and change his bandages."

"Right away, Doc," Larry said. "Cap'n Garrison's still out on patrol, but he'll certainly be glad to get this news when he returns. Luke, it's sure good to have you back with us."

"Thanks, Larry."

"Lieutenant, now that you've regained con-sciousness, it's going to be painful when I remove the bandages and clean out your wounds," Mathis said. "However, there is still the possibility of infection, until they are kept completely closed, and clean. I also have to make certain the skin over the wounds doesn't heal before the internal damage. If it does, and seals one of the wounds shut, there's a good chance a pocket of infection would form under the skin, which could eventually burst, and possibly spread the infection again, putting your life back in danger."

He pulled back the sheet covering Luke's lower body, and began unwrapping the bandage from around Luke's right thigh.

"I'm trying to work as gently as I can," he said.

"It's not all that bad, Doc," Luke answered. "At least not compared to taking a bullet."

"I would imagine," Mathis answered.

"Doc, how long am I gonna be laid up?" Luke asked.

"Right now, that's hard to say. It will be several weeks, at least. While the break in your humerus bone was, luckily, not a serious one, and the bone wasn't shattered, your body still needs a good amount of time for the bone to knit itself back together. Unfortunately, there's no possible way to speed up the process. Every individual recuperates at his or her own pace, of course, but it will be at least six to eight weeks before you'll regain anything near full use of your arm."

"How about shooting a gun?"

"Again, it's a matter of time. You're young, Lieutenant, and in relatively good physical condition, both of which are helpful. Unless unforeseen complications set in, you should regain full use of the arm, and be able to use a weapon with as much speed and accuracy as you did prior to your injury. That said, you'll need to wait a minimum of three or four weeks before you start exercising your arm. If you attempt to rush your recovery, the bone could easily fracture again, possibly even more severely than the first break. If that happens, there is a good chance your arm will be permanently crippled. I know this is something you don't want to hear, Lieutenant, but you'll be out of action for the foreseeable future. You won't even be able to get out of that cot for the next week; then, you should be able to move to your own tent, but you'll still be required to remain in bed for at least another week after that. Knowing you as well as I do, I realize I'm talking to a brick wall, but you'll have to be patient. Let Mother Nature work her magic, and allow her to heal you in her own good time."

"That's easy for you to say, Doc."

"I know that. However, if you'd like some good news, the wound to your leg is healing nicely. I'm going to put some more dressing on it, replace the bandages, then go to work on your arm."

Mathis kept working, carefully removing the splint from Luke's arm, changing the bandages and dressing, then resplinting the arm and putting it back in a sling.

"Your arm's coming along nicely, too," he said, once he was finished. "Now to get at that belly wound."

Once again, Mathis went through the motions

of removing the old bandages from around Luke's belly, cleaning and redressing the wound, then wrapping fresh bandages around Luke's middle.

"This is exactly what I wanted to see, Lieutenant," he said, as he tied the last knot in place. "There is no swelling, heat, or redness around the wound, except for the new skin which is forming. Now, all you need to do is rest, and allow your body to heal itself. That, and we still have to be cautious not to break the stitches before they're ready to come out. I won't be able to remove them until a week to ten days from now. Once those are out, and you're strong enough, I'm going to send you home to finish your recuperation."

"Home?" Luke said.

"Yes, home," Mathis replied. "I'm a bit puzzled. You don't seem pleased by that. Is that a problem?"

"Nope, not at all. I guess it's just a bit of a surprise. It's gonna take a while for the news to settle in."

"That's understandable, especially since you've just regained consciousness after a week and a half," Mathis said. "It will take a few days for your brain to return to functioning normally. In case you're wondering why I'm sending you home to finish your recuperation, there's no real need to keep you here. I'm positive you'll recover more rapidly at home, anyway, with the support of your family and friends. Your own physician will be able to handle any medical needs that might arise. I'll send instructions for your care to him along with you. I've already cleared medical leave with Captain Garrison. Your position will be held until you're fully recovered, and able to return to work."

"I appreciate that, Doc," Luke said. "I reckon I've also gotta say I'm obliged to you for savin' my life. It *will* be good to see my wife and kids again, and have more'n a few days to spend with them before I have to ride out once more. Almost makes takin' a few bullets worth it."

"I wouldn't go quite that far, Lieutenant," Mathis answered. "As far as my saving your life, that's what I'm paid, and trained, to do. The men in your patrol had as much a part in your survival as I did. Had they not done such a good job of treating your wounds, and gotten you here as quickly as they did, you would have died well before I ever had the chance to operate. God took a hand, too. Without Him looking after you, you'd be with the angels right now."

"Or the devils," Luke said, managing a soft chuckle.

Larry stepped back inside the tent. He was carrying a tin bowl of broth, and a canteen of water.

"Someone here order the soup *du jour*?" he asked.

"That would be this gentleman right here," Mathis answered. "Lieutenant, Larry and I will help you sit up. I want you to take this broth slowly. You also need to stop eating, as soon as you feel full. Since it's been quite a while since you took any nourishment, in addition to the bullet wound, it will take a few days for your digestive tract to adjust. You'll most likely feel some discomfort; nausea, gas, bloating, or even a slight bellyache. However, if you experience any sharp, stabbing pain in your lower gut, stop eating, immediately. That could indicate there is still leakage from your bowels, which means I would need to go back in and operate again. If you're ready, we'll sit you up now. If you need assistance eating, we'll help with that."

"I'm more than ready, Doc," Luke answered. "I feel as hollowed out as an old log."

"Having an appetite is another sign of progress," Mathis answered. "Let's see how much you can keep down."

Luke surprised Mathis by downing the entire bowl of broth, plus half the water in the canteen.

"That's very good, Lieutenant. Excellent, in fact," he said. "Now, I know this will sound rather silly, since you've just awakened after so much time, but you do need some more rest. I'm going to give you a dose of laudanum to help you sleep."

"That sounds more than just silly. I'm not at all

sleepy. Well, maybe just a little," Luke answered.

"You just let me be the doctor, so you can get better, and return to Rangering as quickly as possible," Mathis said. "One more good night's sleep will do wonders for you."

"All right," Luke conceded. "I'm not in any shape to fight you, anyway."

"No, you're not," Mathis said, with a smile. He took down a bottle, uncorked it, and filled a tablespoon with some of its contents.

"Here you go," he said, as he put the spoon to Luke's mouth. Luke swallowed the bitter liquid and grimaced.

"Hell, Doc, that stuff burns worse'n the bullets I took. What're you tryin' to do, finish the job the Spencer gang couldn't?"

"I've got stuff here that would finish you off much faster than laudanum, or a bullet," Mathis answered, as he filled the spoon again. "No, I'm merely helping you go back to sleep. Here, just one more spoonful."

Luke shook his head, but then took the medicine.

"You'll feel the effects momentarily," he said.

"No, it's working already," Luke said. On his still mostly empty stomach, the laudanum was rapidly taking effect. His eyelids were growing heavy, and he yawned.

"That's as it should," Mathis said. "I'll see you in the morning, Lieutenant. Larry will be here to call me if I'm needed before then."

"All right. I'm not goin' anywhere."

Luke's voice trailed off, and his eyes closed.

"Boy howdy, that worked fast," Larry said.

"I intended it to. That's why I gave him a double dose," Mathis answered. "I'm going back to finish my supper. Call me if you need me, Larry."

"Sure thing, Doc."

Once Mathis left, Larry settled back into his chair, stretched out his legs, and pulled his hat down over his eyes.

"Since everybody else is asleep in here, there's no reason I shouldn't grab some shut-eye too," he murmured.

Two weeks later, Luke had become strong enough to ride home, where he would finish his recuperation. He was sitting in Captain Shaver's tent, waiting while the captain signed his furlough papers. With them was Major John B. Jones, the Commanding Officer of the Frontier Battalion. Jones was making one of his regular visits to Company D, along with the other companies of the Battalion.

"Lieutenant, I'm certainly pleased I arrived here in time to visit with you before you left," Jones said.

"It's always good to see you, Major Jones," Luke answered.

"Thank you. I just want to repeat what Captain Shaver has already told you. You and your men did an excellent piece of work in bringing Matt Spencer and his outlaw band to justice. They'd been preying on the decent citizens of this area for far too long now. It's unfortunate that two good men died bringing an end to their depredations, but, as we all know, sadly, death is all too common for any man attempting to uphold the law in Texas."

"I appreciate that, Major. Thank you."

"Also, your position as an officer in good standing with the Frontier Battalion will remain in effect while you are recovering. As soon as you are able to return to work, send a message to myself or Captain Garrison. While I'm certain you'd like to remain at home with your family for as long as possible, we need you back in service badly, so I hope your recuperation is a speedy one."

"I understand, Major. I'm obliged."

"Good. Captain Shaver, are the lieutenant's papers signed?"

"Just finished," Shaver answered. He passed one copy to Luke.

"Here you go, Lieutenant. Don't try'n push yourself goin' home," he said. "Doc Mathis said you're to take things easy, so don't be tryin' to get home in a couple of days."

"It's not all that far to Junction," Luke

answered. "It's an easy three day ride. If there's nothing else, I'd like to get started."

"There's not," Shaver answered. "*Vaya con Dios.*"

"Godspeed, Lieutenant," Jones added.

"*Gracias*, both of you. *Adios.*"

Luke went out to where his horses were already saddled and waiting. Joe Driscoll was lying on the ground, head pillowed on his saddle, his shirt unbuttoned while he let the hot rays of the sun soothe his still healing chest wound.

"You on your way, Luke?" he asked.

"Yep. I'll be home in three days. It's sure gonna be good to see Addie and my kids again."

"I'd imagine," Joe said. "You take it easy."

"You too, Joe. I'll see you in a month or two."

"If I'm here when you get back. The doc tells me I'll be back in the saddle in two weeks, at most. That means I'll most likely be out on patrol when you return."

"That's good to hear, Joe. *Adios.*"

"*Adios*, Luke."

Doctor Mathis was waiting with Luke's horses.

"I just want to observe you mount, and ride for a short distance, Lieutenant," he told Luke. "I want to be certain you'll be able to do that without putting excess strain on your right arm or leg."

"That won't be a problem," Luke answered.

"I've ridden in worse shape than this, more'n once."

Pete and RePete nuzzled their owner, begging for a treat. Luke pulled a half-dried out carrot from his hip pocket, broke it in half, and gave a piece to each horse, with a pat to their necks.

"Time to get goin', pardners," he said to them. He would be riding RePete the first day, while Pete carried the pack saddle and supplies. Luke checked his cinches one final time, grasped the saddle horn with his left hand, put his left foot in the stirrup, and pulled himself into the saddle, not using his right arm, which was still splinted and in a sling, at all.

"See, Doc. No trouble at all," he said, grinning. He walked, then trotted, RePete in a tight circle. "No issue ridin', either."

"Lieutenant, from what I've just seen, I can't dispute that," Mathis agreed. "Please, don't ride too hard and strain something on your way home. Once you arrive there, see your doctor as soon as possible. He'll need to check that you didn't aggravate your injuries on the ride. You already have the instructions I wrote out for you. Make certain he gets a copy. Once the splint is removed from your arm, you'll be able to start exercising it, to bring it back to strength. Just make certain not to rush things, and overdo it. A strain, muscle pull, or worse, rebreaking the bone, will set you back at least a month. If all goes the way I expect, you'll be able to return to duty in about six weeks."

"I'm hopin' for a month at most, Doc."

"It's possible, but unlikely. You'll have to see how you progress. Good luck, and good-bye."

"*Adios*, Doc. Thanks for everything."

Luke put RePete into a walk, with Pete following behind. The twin paints had a strong bond with each other, and with Luke, so there was no need to tie Pete's lead rope to Luke's saddle. Instead, it was looped around Pete's neck. He would follow close behind Luke, alongside him where the trail was wide enough.

Luke waved to Beau Billings, who was the sentry on duty, then pushed his horse into a faster walk.

I'm goin' home, he thought.

As soon as he was out of sight of the camp, Luke put RePete into a steady lope, a ground covering gait that was easy on the horse, and comfortable as a rocking chair for his rider.

"We're gonna be home in time for dinner on Thursday, boys," he said. Both horses snorted, as if in agreement.

Chapter 4

Luke reached the outskirts of his home town of Junction in the middle of the afternoon, three days later. He was riding alongside the Llano River, softly humming a random tune. As he passed a large limestone outcropping opposite the riverbank, a shrill war cry split the air. A slight figure leapt from the top of the rocks, landed on RePete's rump, and wrapped its arms around Luke's waist.

"Pa! You're back!" his ten-year-old son, John, screamed. "Why didn't you let us know you were comin' home? What happened to your arm? How long are you stayin' this time?"

"Whoa, easy. Rein in there and slow down a bit, Johnny boy. One question at a time," Luke answered. "You scared me out of ten years of my life, jumping outta the brush like that. You're lucky I didn't mistake you for a bushwhacker, and shoot you dead. How'd you spot me?"

"Gee whillikers, I'm sure sorry, Pa. I just got so excited when I saw you comin' I couldn't wait, that's all. Me, Jack Hooper, and Tommy Donegan were swimmin' in the river. When I seen you comin', I wanted to surprise you. So real quick, I threw my clothes back on, and scrambled up in the rocks. I got hidden before you knew I was there."

"Saw me comin'," Luke corrected.

"Okay, Pa. When I saw you comin', I decided to hide, then jump out and surprise you. I didn't mean nothin' by it."

"Anythin' by it."

"Anythin' by it. You ain't mad at me, are you, Pa?"

"Of course not. You gave me a great welcome home. I didn't let your ma know I was on the way back, because I wanted to surprise all of you. My arm got busted during a gunfight with some real bad *hombres*. I'll be stayin' home until it heals up, so at least a month, mebbe a bit more. Listen, don't be yellin' I'm comin' when we ride into town. I still want to surprise your ma."

"I won't make a sound, Pa," Johnny promised.

"Good. How's Ma doin'? And your sisters and brother?"

"They're all doin' fine, I guess. Molly and Debbie are over to the Malones, visiting with Jenny and Annie. Donnie's at Billy Tucker's house. Ma's busy as ever. We all help her as much as we can."

"I'm glad to hear that. I know it's hard with me away from home so much. I appreciate you kids helpin' her out."

"We don't mind. It's fun, most of the time, especially when we deliver the papers and sometimes folks give us a penny for licorice. Boy

71

howdy, they'll all sure be happy to see you come home."

"No more happy that I will to be home," Luke said. "Let's hush up now, just so your ma doesn't overhear us when we reach our place."

"All right, Pa."

Luke looked around as he and his son rode along Junction's main street. The town was little changed since he had left, nearly five months previously. A number of passersby waved to him and Johnny, or shouted greetings, while he walked his horses down the middle of the street, then reined up in front of the building which stood next to the office of the local newspaper, the *Junction Clarion.*

"Stay out here with the horses for a couple of minutes, Johnny," Luke said, as the boy slid off RePete's rump, and Luke dismounted. "Take 'em over to the trough, and let 'em have a short drink. Not too much, until they've cooled off some. We don't want them to founder, or colic. I'd like to surprise your mother by myself."

"Sure, Pa. You're gonna be huggin' and kissin' on her anyways, and all that mushy stuff. Yuck. I sure don't need to see that. Who wants to kiss a dumb girl, anyhow? Phooey!"

Luke laughed.

"You wait a couple more years, Johnny boy, and you'll know why. You'll change your mind, mark my words."

"That'll never happen," Johnny answered. "Girls are too silly."

He spat in the dirt.

"Just you wait and see," Luke said. "Go on, get outta here."

"All right." Johnny took RePete's and Pete's reins. "C'mon, boys, time for a drink." He led them away, while Luke climbed the stairs in front of the *Clarion*, crossed the boardwalk, opened the door, and stepped inside. Adeline, his wife, was in the back, hunched over a drawer as she selected letters to be set into a composing stick, in preparation for printing that week's edition of the paper. She was so engrossed in her work she didn't hear the tinkle of the bell attached to the door, which let her know when a customer walked in.

"Stop the press!" Luke shouted. "New headline. Texas Ranger Luke Caldwell has returned home."

Startled, Adeline jumped, then whirled around, dropping type and scattering it across the floor. She clapped both hands to her face in surprise.

"Luke!" She ran across the room and threw herself into his grasp. He wrapped his left arm around her and hugged her tightly, then pressed his lips to hers in a long, lingering kiss, which ended only when she pulled back, to catch her breath.

"Luke! I can't believe it. I'm so happy to see you. The children will be pleased and excited, too. Why didn't you send a telegram that you were coming home? And what happened to your arm?"

"Wait for a minute, and I'll tell you. I want to just look at you first."

Luke stepped back, and ran his gaze up and down Adeline's curvaceous figure. She wore an ink stained printer's apron over her pink checked gingham dress, which only emphasized the soft roundness of her breasts, and the gentle curves of her hips. To Luke, a smudge of ink on the tip of her slightly turned up nose simply highlighted her peaches and cream skin, making her even more desirable. She pushed a strand of auburn hair from where it had fallen over her emerald green eyes, pushing it back in place. Luke's exhaustion seemed to disappear, as the blood began racing through his veins. After months of separation, the desire to feel Addie's body pressed against his was not to be denied. He fought hard against the churning in his belly, the stirring in his groin, and the urge to take her, right then and there.

"Honey, you look better, and more beautiful, every time I see you. Boy howdy, I've missed you, Addie."

"Not as much as I've missed you. Now, enough stalling. Tell me why your arm's in a sling. And you've got some nerve, not letting me know you were on the way home."

"Me and some of the men got into a little

dustup with an outlaw gang, that's all. A bullet hit my arm and nicked the bone. Our company doc says it'll be at least a month before it heals up and I can really use it again, so here I am. I didn't send a wire because I wanted to surprise you and the kids."

"Is that the entire story?"

"Not exactly," Luke admitted. "I'll tell you everything a little later, once the kids are home, so I don't have to tell it twice. Johnny met me on the way in. He took the horses to give 'em a drink. I've got to take care of them before I do anything else. Besides, don't you have to finish getting the paper ready?"

"The paper! I was so thrilled to see you walk through the door I nearly forgot. Yes, and just look what you made me do. I had the entire front page almost set, then you waltzed in, and shocked me so badly I dropped type all over the floor. Now I've got to pick it up, sort it out, and reset all the lines."

"I'm sorry, Addie. I'll give you a hand getting things straightened out."

"No, but thank you. It won't take me all that long. While I fix this mess, take care of your horses. Once you've cared for them, and cleaned up a bit yourself, supper will be almost ready. The paper doesn't come out until tomorrow, so I'll just reset the pages today, then get up early and print it in the morning."

"As long as you're certain."

"I am. Besides, we have all night to make up for the past several months."

The glint in Addie's eyes and the promise in her smile told Luke she was as eager to spend the night in the same bed as he was. Weeks of separation from the one she loves will do that to a woman. And for a man like Luke, who had promised to remain faithful to his wife on their wedding day, and not ever lay with another woman, keeping that promise could be physically painful. Diving into a frigid river or dunking his head into a cold bucket of water offered little, inadequate relief. However, despite the many opportunities he had available to break his vow while away from home, he had never given into temptation, but remained faithful to Adeline. Over time, he learned that keeping his promise made his homecomings that much sweeter. The anticipation was almost as thrilling as the lovemaking itself. He swallowed hard before speaking once more.

"I can hardly wait to have some of your good cookin' again," he said. "Bacon and beans over a campfire, or greasy food in a dingy café, sure gets tiresome before long. What's for supper?"

"Roast beef, boiled potatoes, black-eyed peas, and I baked an apple pie only this morning," Addie answered.

"Just what I was hopin' you'd say," Luke

answered. "It won't take me long to be ready." He gave her a quick kiss on the cheek. "Love you."

"I love you also, but I need to get this paper set," Addie said. She gave him a slap on his butt. "Go tend to your horses so I can get my work finished."

"Yes, ma'am!" Luke said. He gave her another quick kiss, then headed back outside.

The Caldwell family's living quarters were in the same building as the *Clarion*, separated by a solid door, with a living room, kitchen, and pantry downstairs, and three bedrooms on the second floor. Behind the building, at the far edge of the back yard, was the outhouse, and, beyond that, the small stable and adjoining corral where Luke kept his horses. He, with Johnny's help, had taken the gear off the mounts, put them in their stalls, watered and grained them. They were now grooming Pete and RePete while the tired animals munched on hay. Pete leaned hard into the currycomb Luke held, and nuzzled Luke's face.

"I know, I'm glad to be home, too," he said, when the gelding nickered. "Johnny, how're you comin' with RePete?"

"I'd be almost done, if this doggone horse would just stand still, and stop tryin' to lick my face," Johnny answered.

Luke laughed.

"He's just glad to see you, that's all. RePete always did take to you, from the day I brought him home."

Luke turned when he heard his youngest child, Donald, come running into the barn. With him was the family dog, a big, shaggy, white and tan spotted mixed breed named Scout.

"Howdy, Pa! Ma said you were home." The boy ran up to Luke and jumped into his outstretched left arm. Tears of happiness ran down the seven year old's cheeks as he hugged his father tightly. Scout cavorted around them, barking with joy, his tail wagging wildly.

"Howdy yourself, Donnie. Hey, what're you cryin' for? I'm home, and I'm stayin' home for a while. There's no need for tears."

"I know, Pa. I'm so happy to see you, I just couldn't help it, I guess," Donnie said. "I'm sorry."

"There's no need to be sorry," Luke said. "A man shouldn't be ashamed to cry, if he's got a reason. I've cried plenty of times when I've lost a friend, especially a friend who gets himself killed fightin' renegades. I cried when your grandma and grandpa died, too. Heck, I even cry when I see a horse die."

"You do?"

"I sure do, son. Tell you what. Give me and Johnny a hand rubbin' down the horses, then we'll have some time to catch up before supper. All right?"

"Sure, Pa."

Donnie grabbed a soft brush and started working on Pete, brushing dirt and sweat out of his legs and fetlocks.

Fifteen minutes later, the horses were settled for the night. Luke patted each on the neck, and gave them a piece of licorice.

"Good night, pards," he told the horses. "You've got a few weeks of doin' nothin' but hangin' around, gettin' fat and lazy, ahead. Boy howdy, you both sure deserve it."

Luke and his boys washed up at the pump and trough behind the barn, then went inside the house and straight to the kitchen.

"Ma, we're here," Donny hollered, at the top of his lungs. "Is supper ready? I'm plumb starved. We all are, even Scout."

"Donnie, how many times do I have to remind you not to scream like a banshee indoors?" Addie said. "No, supper is not ready. Your sisters will be home by five o'clock, which is less than twenty minutes from now. It will be ready by then. You'll just have to wait."

"Pa, do we have to wait until after we eat to hear about how you got shot? Can't you tell us now?" Johnny pleaded.

"Yeah, Pa, c'mon. We want to hear the story," Donnie added.

"Go ahead and tell them," Addie said. "I'd rather hear what happened sooner than later. But please, try not to embellish the story in the telling, at least not *too* much. You know how you like to exaggerate."

"I'll do my best, but I can't promise anything," Luke answered, then laughed. "All right, boys, here goes. Me 'n six other men were sent out after an outlaw gang, which was led by a man name of Matt Spencer. Spencer was one of the meanest *hombres* ever to walk the face of the Earth. Most of the men with him were just as bad. They'd been robbin' and killin' folks for months, all over west Texas. We'd been trailin' 'em for weeks, and finally had 'em trapped in a canyon, right alongside the Rio Grande."

"So what happened?" Donnie asked.

"Be patient, Donnie. I'm getting to that," Luke answered. "We were expectin' Spencer and his bunch to try'n catch us in an ambush, and sure enough, they'd set one up. They were hidin' in the rocks atop an old landslide, just waitin' for us to ride into range. Luckily, one of my men, a brand new Ranger named Joe Driscoll, caught sight of one of 'em. That spoiled the trap they'd planned. Joe got shot durin' the fight that followed, but he's gonna be all right."

"How'd you get outta bein' drygulched, even with the warning?" Johnny asked. "Seems to me the outlaws had the advantage, bein' on the high ground, and takin' cover behind rocks, while you and your men were out in the open."

"Hold on, and I'll tell you."

"Boys, please, just let your father tell his story," Addie said. "If you keep interrupting him, you'll never hear the ending."

"All right, Ma," Donnie said. "Go ahead, Pa. We'll keep quiet."

"Thanks. Anyway, since there was no way to circle around behind those *hombres*, we had two choices. We could turn tail and run, or we could fight."

"And Texas Rangers never run from a fight, right, Pa?" Donnie said.

"That's right. Now, besides havin' the better cover, up in the rocks on a ridge at the top of the slide, Spencer's gang also outnumbered us, two to one. The only advantage we had was surprise, since they didn't have any idea we knew they were waitin' for us. So, we galloped our horses as fast as we could, firin' our rifles at the outlaws while we rode lickety-split for cover, then jumped off 'em and dove into the brush and rocks at the bottom of the slide. The trick worked, because by the time those *hombres* realized we'd fooled 'em, and started shootin' at us, we were already in cover. Before they even gave me a chance to ask 'em to surrender, one of those skunks tried to take a shot at me. I didn't give him the chance to pull his trigger. I took a quick shot, and *Pow!*

I let him have it, right between his eyes. That meant one less to worry about."

"Wow! Then what?" Johnny said. Both boys were hanging on Luke's every word.

"I yelled up to Matt Spencer, to try'n talk him and his men into givin' up. He just laughed. My sergeant, Ben Thibodeaux, nailed another man who got careless, and showed himself. That started the whole outfit into shootin' at us. We had to fight our way up the hill to clean out that nest of rattlesnakes."

"I bet it was some kind of a fight," Donnie exclaimed.

"Boy howdy, it sure was," Luke said. "We couldn't even watch out for each other, the bullets were rainin' down so hard. I killed two men before I got hit, shot one in the chest, the other one clean through his guts. Then, one of the other outlaws shot me in my right leg. That dropped me to one knee. I took a shot at him, but I missed. When I did, *Bang!* He let me have it, right in my belly."

"You got plugged in the belly?" Donnie exclaimed, his eyes wide in disbelief.

"I sure did, Donnie boy. Plumb through my guts. But I finished off the *hombre* who got me with my next bullet. That one didn't miss. I drilled him right through his ribs. He went down and didn't get back up."

"But how'd you keep on fightin', Pa, with

slugs in your leg and belly?" Johnny asked.

"It wasn't easy. I was hurt real bad, and could barely stand. But I knew if I quit, and just laid down, I'd never have made it. So I struggled my way up the slide. When I reached the ridge where the outlaws were hidin', most of the other Rangers had already gotten there. A whole passel of the outlaws were already dead, or wounded bad enough they were out of the fight. I shot my rifle until it ran out of bullets, then tossed it aside and pulled out my six-gun. One man came at me with a knife. I tried to shoot him in the chest, but my bullet hit the knife instead. He kept comin' at me anyway, so I stuck the barrel of my Colt right smack in the middle of his belly, and put two bullets through him. By then, the fight was almost over, but one of the outlaws who was still fightin' tried to shoot me in the back. Ed Dunleavy, another of my men, shot him just as he pulled the trigger, and ruined his aim, so that's the *hombre* whose bullet broke my arm. After that, the fight was just about done. Good thing, too, because I couldn't have kept goin' much longer. I checked on the other boys, then a couple of the men patched me up, until we could get back to camp, where Doc Mathis dug the bullet out of my belly, and fixed up my arm and leg. Once I was strong enough to ride, I headed for home to finish healin' up."

"What happened to the renegades?" Johnny

asked. "And were any other Rangers hurt, or killed?"

"None of those *hombres* would give up, so they're all dead," Luke answered. He shook his head. "We lost two men, Sergeant Thibodeaux, and a young Ranger named Shep Hawkins. I already mentioned Joe Driscoll, who was hit in the chest, but is comin' along just fine. The only other Ranger who got hit was Ed Dunleavey. He took a bullet in his rump."

"You mean someone shot him in his behind?" Donnie said.

"Yep, they sure did. Listen, I've told you this before, but I'll say it again. Sure, ridin' all over Texas, chasin' down bad guys, sounds exciting, but it's not. What it is, is hard, dirty work, with way too much time in the saddle, too much bad food, and too little rest, for nowhere near enough pay, and never knowin' when a bullet might have your name on it. The only reason I got into Rangerin' is I was tired of lookin' at the south end of north bound cows for hundreds of miles, drivin' them on their way to Kansas and the railroads. Since cowboyin' was all I knew, but I was pretty handy with a gun, I tried for a job with the Rangers, and they put me on. I won't tell you boys not to become lawmen when you grow up, if that's what you want, but I sure hope you'll find somethin' better'n that. Mebbe take over the newspaper from your ma some day."

"Aw, but Pa. I wanna be a lawman, just like you," Johnny said.

"So do I," Donnie added.

"Wait until you grow up, then we'll see," Addie told them.

"Pa, can I see your bullet holes?" Donnie asked.

Luke laughed.

"Well, there's not a lot to see, since they've pretty much healed."

"But I still want to see 'em. Please, Pa?"

"I want to see 'em, too," Johnny added.

"Well, you can't see the one in my arm, since I won't be able to remove the splints for another week," Luke answered. "And I'm sure not gonna drop my britches right here in the kitchen to show you the one in my leg."

"How about the one in your belly?" Donnie insisted.

Luke looked at Addie.

"Go ahead," she told him. "You might as well get it over with. They're bound to see it sooner or later, in any event."

Luke sighed.

"All right."

He undid the bottom three buttons of his shirt, then opened it, to reveal the still livid wound.

Donnie gave a choked gurgle, then swallowed hard, and took a closer look. Johnny stared at the wound, in rapt fascination.

"Oh boy, Pa," he said. "I'd bet my hat that must've hurt somethin' awful."

"It still does, although not as bad as it did," Luke said, as he rebuttoned his shirt. "It'll probably bother me for a long time, mebbe even the rest of my life. Getting shot for real isn't like when you're playin' cowboys and Indians. It's not pretend, where you act like you've been killed, then a minute later get right back up and start shootin' again. If a real bullet hits you in your vitals, you most likely are gonna die, sometimes slow and painful. I'm just lucky God was watchin' over me, and that Doc Mathis is a real fine surgeon. Otherwise, I wouldn't be here with you and your ma right now."

"I still want to be a lawman like you," Johnny insisted. "At least if I do die in a gunfight, I'll die tryin' to help honest folks."

"Same goes for me," Donnie said.

"That's admirable, but you'll need to wait until you're older, and still certain that's what you want," Addie said.

"Besides, things are changin', even for lawmen," Luke said. "We're whittlin' down the numbers of outlaws out there. More and more, crimes are solved by investigation, not with fists and guns. By the time you boys are old enough to decide what you want to be, you'll need more brains than fightin' ability, to become a lawman, especially a Ranger. Which means you have to study hard, and get good grades."

"I just knew he'd say somethin' about school, Donnie," Johnny said, rolling his eyes and groaning.

Behind the boys, Addie smiled at Luke.

"I couldn't have put it better myself, sweetheart," she said. "That's enough of this conversation. The girls will be home any minute now. Luke, I want you to just sit down and relax. John and Donald, I want you to help me set the table."

"Okay, Ma," Johnny said. "C'mon, Donnie. The sooner we get the dishes on the table, the sooner we can eat."

"If our dumb sisters ever show up," Donnie grumbled. As if on cue, the back door opened. Twelve-year-old Deborah and nine-year-old Molly walked into the kitchen. Both stopped short at the sight of their father, then Molly broke into a run.

"Pa!" she yelled, as she jumped into his lap. "You came home!"

"I sure did, sugar," Luke said. "How's one of my three best gals?"

"I'm just fine, Pa," Molly said. "Can I have a kiss?"

"Of course."

When Luke kissed her, Molly giggled.

"Your beard tickles," she said.

"I'm sorry, Molly. I haven't had the chance to shave, plus with this broken arm it's not all that easy. Tell you what. Why don't you get down, so

I can give Debbie her kiss? I'm gonna be home for at least a month, so we'll all have plenty of time to catch up."

"All right."

Debbie had been waiting patiently. Her eyes were moist with tears of happiness, but her manner was reserved.

"Come here, Debbie, and give your ol' pa a kiss," Luke asked.

"Sure, Pa, I mean, Father. I'm most distressed to see you've been injured."

Debbie kissed him demurely on the cheek. Luke pulled her to him, and gave her a hug.

"I'm so happy to see my big girl again," he said. "Let me take a look at you. Boy howdy, you've grown at least a couple of inches while I've been away. What's the matter, sweetheart? You don't seem happy to see me. Are you mad at me because I was gone so long?"

Whatever reserve Debbie was trying to maintain crumbled. The tears started to flow, while she hugged her father tightly.

"Oh, Pa, I'm not mad at you one bit," she said. "It's just . . . just . . . I'm trying to act more mature now, that's all. I wanted to show you I'm growing up."

"It's okay, Debbie," Luke said, as he stroked her hair. "I can see you're becoming a young lady, but you'll always be my little girl, no matter how old you are."

He gave her another kiss on the cheek.

"Debbie's tryin' to act all snooty and high-falutin' like her new friend, Louisa," Molly said.

"I am not," Debbie shot back.

"You are so," Johnny said. "You don't wrestle anymore, or climb trees, or help me or Donny find worms to go fishin'. You won't catch frogs no more, neither. Heck, you won't even run races nowadays."

"See?" Molly said. She stuck out her tongue at her older sister.

"That's enough, from all of you," Addie said. "We all like doing things differently as we get older. It's time to eat. Johnny, you and your brother finish getting the dishes on the table, while I take the roast out of the oven. Girls, go wash your hands and faces. Supper will be ready by the time you're finished."

"Certainly, Mother," Debbie said.

"See? High-falutin'," Molly insisted, as she ran to the pump and sink. Luke just shook his head and laughed.

Within a few minutes, everyone was seated around the table.

"Luke, since you haven't been home, it's your turn to lead the Grace, unless you'd rather not," Addie said.

"Of course. I'll be happy to give the blessing," Luke answered. "Let's bow our heads and fold our hands as we give thanks to God for the many blessings He has bestowed upon us."

Luke waited for a moment until everyone was ready, then began his prayer.

"We thank Thee, O Lord, for the many blessings You have given this family, the food before us, the roof over our heads, our friends and relations, and most of all, Your abundant love. We also thank You for my safe return to my family, for the continued recovery of Joe Driscoll and Ed Dunleavey, my friends and pardners. We also request You to grant eternal rest with You in Heaven to my deceased friends and pardners, Ben Thibodeaux and Shep Hawkins, who gave up their lives in service to others. Amen."

"Amen."

"Now let's eat!" Donnie exclaimed, reaching for a slice of bread.

"Donald, please remember your manners."

The gentle rebuke came not from Addie, but from his older sister, Debbie.

"All right, now I'm as curious as a cat," Luke said. "Why *have* you become so concerned about manners and such, Debbie?" Luke asked. "It seems more than just growin' up, from my sights."

"Because of my new friend, Louisa. She and her family just moved here from New York City. She knows all about the latest clothing styles, and how people in more civilized cities behave."

"Oh ho," said Luke.

"Perhaps I'd better explain to your father for you, darling," Addie said. "Yes, a new family, the Phillipses, moved to town, about two weeks after you left. They bought the old Delaney house. There's the father, mother, and five children. Louisa is only a few weeks older than Deborah. Her family is quite well-to-do. Mr. Phillips is one of the vice-presidents of a large Eastern land syndicate. He was transferred to Texas because of the company's interest in obtaining ranch lands for their investors."

"It hardly seems folks like that could be happy in a small town like Junction, Texas," Luke said.

"I'm not certain but that you're correct," Addie said. "Maude Phillips has taken it upon herself to teach the young women of this town all the finer points of etiquette. She claims that will help civilize this God-forsaken territory. She's set aside a room in their home, and calls her establishment 'Mrs. Phillips School of Charm, Etiquette, and Decorum for Cultured Young Ladies.' Needless to say, almost every female in town is enthralled with the idea."

"Seems like foolishness to me," Luke said. "Junction ain't New York City. Folks here get by just fine, thank you very much, without someone tellin' 'em to stick out their pinky finger when they drink their tea, or not cuss in front of ladies, or get too drunk and rowdy at a town social."

"It's not foolishness at all, Father," Debbie

said. "Until I met Louisa and her family, I never realized how . . ." she struggled to recall the word she wanted, "how *uncouth* people in this town are. For example, you eat with your elbows on the table, and you shovel your food into your mouth without hardly chewing it. You haven't changed into clean clothes for supper, either. You haven't even bathed or shaved. Your appearance is so unkempt."

"You look just fine to me, Pa," Molly exclaimed.

"Thanks, honey," Luke answered. "As far as you, Debbie, be careful how you talk about Junction, young lady," Luke said. "It's where I was born and raised, and lived my entire life. We have plenty of, what did you call it, *couth* around these parts. Why, your mother came out here all the way from Philadelphia, Pennsylvania. She even graduated from a women's college in Massachusetts, yet she's never once complained about my manners, or tried to change my ways. We're as good here in Junction as any big Eastern city. We just don't get all uppity, that's all. If you really want to learn about those fancy Eastern ways, your mother can teach you every bit as much as this Mrs. Phillips, probably more. And without it costing anything, since I don't imagine Mrs. Phillips is donating her time."

"It's not very expensive, Father."

"Deborah, I believe that's enough of this

discussion," Addie said. "Your father just got back this afternoon. He hasn't had time to take a bath, or shave. Welcoming him home is all you should be concerned with right now. The same goes for you, Luke. I'm just going to say that the tuition for Deborah's lessons is not excessive, and if she wants to improve herself, I see no harm in that. Now, this topic is *verboten* for the rest of the evening."

"Uh-oh. Ma's speaking German again," Johnny said. "She only does that when she's puttin' her foot down."

"That's right," Addie answered. "So just hush up, and eat your supper. Pass me the bowl of potatoes, please."

"Sure, Ma."

"Luke, tell us a bit more about your adventures," Addie said. "The girls weren't here when you told the boys about the fight you were in, and I'm certain they'd like to hear some of the details."

"Of course. You see, it was like this . . ."

Luke wasn't sure which he enjoyed more, the first home cooked meal he had eaten in months, or the banter of his family as they ate. After five months on the trail, he was eager to hear some of the town news, as well as what his wife and children had been up to in his absence.

"Addie, that was the best meal I've had since

I left home," he said, after he swallowed his last forkful of pie, and drained the last of his coffee. "I'm plumb stuffed. I can't eat another bite. Can I help you with the dishes?"

"No, the children and I will handle those," Addie said. "You look exhausted. I want you to relax until we're done. Why don't you just go into the living room and have a smoke? It won't take all that long to clean up in here."

"Okay," Luke answered. "It *has* been a long trip. Later on, before we go to bed, I do want to clean up some more. Debbie, you're doggone right about one thing. I need to clean up, badly, and my clothes are filthy. Tomorrow, I've got to stop by Doc Patterson's, so he can take a look at my hurts. Before I do that, I'll go over to the barber shop for a haircut, shave, and long soak. For tonight, I'll just take a quick bath in the kitchen, while you finish setting your paper, Addie."

"Won't that be difficult, with your bad arm?"

"I'll manage. I can drag the tub out of the pantry all right. Only need one arm for that."

"Nonsense!" Addie retorted. "You'll do no such thing. Johnny, you and your brother get the tub from the pantry for your father. Debbie, you and Molly heat up the kettles for him. Get him the soap, a washcloth, and towel, too. By the time that's done, I'll have the type all set, and ready for printing the paper in the morning. As soon as

I'm finished, it will be time for all of you to go straight to bed. No fooling around, or staying up talking, and chattering like magpies. You're to go right to sleep."

"Yup, Pa's home all right," Johnny said. "Every time he comes back, we have to go to bed early."

"Watch your tongue, young man," Addie scolded. "Now go get that tub."

Luke just smiled.

Water was always scarce in west Texas, so, as in most homes, what passed for a bathtub in the Caldwell house was a round, Number 10 sized zinc laundry tub, filled with a few inches of water. It was always difficult for Luke to squeeze his lanky, six foot plus frame into the small tub, now his broken arm made that doubly difficult. However, finally getting the chance to scrub some of the trail dust and grime out of his skin made the effort worth it. He was washing his hair when Addie stepped behind the sheet which had been hung for privacy. The ink spot on her nose now had several companions across her cheeks and on her chin.

"Do you want some help, cowboy?" she asked, smiling. "The kids are asleep, so we don't have to worry about them."

"I reckon I could use some, at least scrubbing my back," Luke said. "Kinda hard to reach it without a brush."

"I can solve that problem," Addie said. "Hand me the soap and washcloth, please."

"Gladly."

Addie took the bar of Pears' glycerin soap. She lathered her husband's back, then ran the washcloth over his skin in long, smooth strokes.

"How does that feel?"

"Like I've died and gone to Heaven, with the prettiest angel up there."

"Flatterer."

"No, I'm not. I'm telling the truth."

"You only want to get me in your bed, cowboy."

"Well, there is that," Luke admitted.

"I'll have you know I don't sleep with just any man."

"I don't either."

Addie slapped the washcloth across the back of Luke's head.

"You don't sleep with just any man? I hope you don't think of me as a man, Mister."

"No, I meant I don't sleep with just any woman. And there's no possible way anyone could mistake you for a man. Besides, I'm not just any *hombre*."

"You can say that again, but that isn't necessarily a good thing. And I'll have you know, cowboy, I'm not just any *señorita*."

"I'm well aware of that. But are you the right woman for me?"

"I'm not certain. What are you looking for?"

"Let me see. A woman who is sassy, sophisticated, and smart, mebbe one from back East somewhere. She also needs to be pretty, not too skinny, and about my age. Dark reddish hair and green eyes, that sparkle like emeralds. Nicely turned ankles, too. And a sweet smile. You seem to fit the bill. Now, what are you looking for in a man?"

"Well, he should be tall, and muscular. He definitely has to have a flat belly and slim hips. Dark hair, but blue eyes. Deep, crystalline blue eyes. Rugged and handsome. Also, one who knows how to treat a lady with respect, gentleness, and kindness. He also should be able to say the things a woman wants to hear. You seem to meet all my criteria, except perhaps for the handsome part. I could overlook that one flaw, though."

"Well, that's right kindly of you, ma'am," Luke drawled.

"If we're through being silly, I'm done with your back," Addie said. "I need to take a quick bath before coming to bed, too. I smell like ink and newsprint. Why don't you dry yourself off, then wait for me upstairs? I promise I won't be long. Don't worry about emptying the tub. I'll do that."

"I can do it," Luke protested. "It's not as if I were a cripple."

"I realize that, but why take a chance on

straining something, particularly tonight," Addie replied.

"I'm not in the mood to argue with you, but I am gonna hold you to that promise not to take too long," Luke warned her.

"You don't have to worry about that," Addie assured him.

While Addie heated more water, Luke got out of the tub, toweled off, wrapped the towel around his waist, and headed upstairs, to his and Addie's bedroom. He dropped the towel on the floor, laid on his back, and stretched out naked on the mattress, with his left arm behind his head, and the broken right one across his chest.

While he waited for Addie, Luke thought back on how they had first met. He had been a Texas Ranger for less than a year, and had just returned home for a short leave. He walked into the *Clarion*'s office to purchase a copy of that week's paper. Instead of William Mulvey, who had established the newspaper, there was a young woman behind the counter, with her back toward him. When she heard Luke's footsteps, she turned to greet him. As soon as he saw her face, his heart seemed to leap into his throat. She was undoubtedly the most attractive woman he had ever seen. A week later, he worked up the courage to ask her to supper, fully expecting to be shot out of the saddle. Instead, she had accepted his invitation.

Over their meal, they had talked for hours, Luke telling Addie about his life as a cowboy, then a lawman, Addie fascinating him with the story of her upbringing. Her full name was Adeline Edith Brockton, the sixth of seven children, one of only two girls. Her parents were wealthy, her father having made his fortune in banking, while her mother was the sole heir to a textile manufacturer's estate. Addie was privileged to attend the Mount Holyoke Female Seminary in Massachusetts, one of the few colleges for women. Needless to say, the Brocktons were prominent members of Philadelphia society. However, Addie was stifled by the demands of high society, and the rules it imposed, especially on women. Despite her parents' objections, she managed to convince them to loan her enough money to travel west, and to start a business if she settled on one suitable. After several months exploring the southwestern United States, she came to Junction, where the owner of the *Clarion* was attempting to sell the paper and retire. Having taken journalism and English classes at Mount Holyoke, Addie immediately bought the weekly.

Despite their entirely different family back-grounds, Luke and Addie felt an immediate, and powerful, attraction, one strong enough for Addie to overcome her loneliness during Luke's long absences, and for Luke to appreciate her independent streak and unconventional—for a woman—ways. In fact, he admired her spunk in standing up to the town gossips, when they complained about her wearing men's denims, or riding astraddle, rather than sidesaddle, as "proper" ladies were supposed to do. In less than two weeks, they were married. On their wedding night, Luke learned another of Addie's secrets. This prim, sophisticated, soft-spoken Eastern woman was a wildcat in bed. She taught him things he had never learned from the soiled doves at the sporting houses and "wayward ladies" homes. Now, waiting for her, Luke grinned at the anticipation of what tonight would bring. He had never broken his promise to remain faithful to Addie the day they wed, no matter how hard resisting temptation might be. Besides, he knew no other woman could give him the exquisite physical pleasure that Addie provided. His reverie broke at the sound of her voice.

"I'm here, darling," she said. "I hope I didn't keep you waiting too long."

"Even a minute waiting for you is too long," Luke answered.

"Perhaps I can make it up to you."

Addie slipped out of the thin robe she wore, dropped it to the floor, and stood at the foot of their bed. Her pale skin seemed to glow in the dim light from the turned-low lamp. Luke gazed at her in admiration of the slow rise and fall of her round, full breasts, appreciating her womanly curves as if he were seeing them for the first time.

"Do you approve?"

"I sure do. You're just as beautiful as the day I first laid eyes on you, if not more so."

"You're every bit as handsome as you were on our wedding night," Addie said. "However, I hope having your arm in that sling won't be a problem."

"I'd rather think of it as a challenge," Luke said. "While I've been waiting, I gave it some thought. I can't put my arm under your back, because that might snap the bone, which obviously is still knitting. But if I put it between us, the same thing could happen."

Addie sat alongside Luke, and ran her fingertips along his ribs.

"You've just described the problem. What about a solution?"

"It's simple. We'll merely have to do things opposite from the way we normally do. You'll be on top, I'll be on the bottom. That way, I can wrap both arms around you and rest them on your back. There's practically no chance of reinjuring my arm if we make love that way."

"What about this?" Addie asked. "Will it bother you?"

When she touched the still healing bullet wound

in Luke's belly, his stomach muscles tightened. He groaned, but not from pain.

"Does it still hurt?" Addie asked, worry in her voice.

"Um . . . no, not exactly. In fact, pretty much the opposite."

Addie touched the wound again. The stirring in Luke's groin made his meaning quite plain.

"Well, Mister Texas Ranger, since it appears you're just about ready, we may as well get started."

Addie took her fingertips, and gently traced a path across Luke's flesh, from the bullet wound, up his belly and chest to his left nipple, over to his right one, than diagonally back to his belly button. She ran her fingers around its rim, then lowered herself gently onto her husband. Luke's tongue flicked at the base of her throat, then he pulled her more tightly to him, and molded his body to hers.

After weeks of separation, Luke and Addie's reunion started off hard and fast, then settled into a long, slow session of tender lovemaking, taking delight in exploring each other's body, rediscovering the points which brought the most pleasure. Their lovemaking lasted well into the early morning. Now, Luke and Addie were lying next to each other, their bodies still glistening with sweat.

"Luke, I know we've talked about what might happen before, but this is the first time you've actually been shot," Addie said. "I didn't realize just how frightening it would be."

"I know," Luke said. "However, I'm here and doing fine. Plus, being shot means we'll have more time together, until I return to duty. Does my taking a couple of bullets change your mind about being married to a fiddle-footed lawman?"

"Not at all," Addie answered, lying her head on his chest. "I've always realized, sooner or later, you'd probably come home wounded . . . or not at all. I've accepted that fact, hard as it may be. And as you pointed out, we'll have more time together while you recuperate. That will make the kids happy, too. And we've talked about how being a newspaper editor in a small frontier town can also be a dangerous occupation. Just a few weeks ago, the owner of a paper up in the Panhandle was shot to death from ambush, and his paper's office burned to the ground. That could happen to me."

"No one would dare try that," Luke said. "One, you're not a woman to be trifled with, and I taught you how to shoot real well. Two, you're also married to a Texas Ranger. Anyone who harmed even one hair on your head knows I'd chase them through Hell and back, and wouldn't quit until they were behind bars . . . or dead."

"My hero," Addie said, and slapped Luke on

his arm. "Just like you are to the boys. It will do them some good to have you around. They need a father's influence. So do the girls, but not so much as the boys."

"I'll be glad to have some time with them. But what's the story with Debbie? She sure has changed. Why has she become so uppity?"

"It's just a phase she's going through, like most girls her age," Addie answered. "She's influenced by all her friends, and that new family in town is unique. She just wants to fit in. She'll get over it."

"I hope so," Luke answered. "I hope she realizes she won't be getting married until she's at least fifty . . . or older."

"You can't keep her your baby girl forever, sweetheart," Addie replied.

"No, but I can sure try. Meantime, I suppose we should get some sleep. I need to get to town early tomorrow."

After breakfast the next morning, Luke headed to Art's Tonsorial Parlor, for a much needed shave, haircut, and bath. He was two blocks from the shop when Russ Cowan, who owned a hardscrabble ranch north of Junction, stepped out of the saddle shop and stopped in front of him, blocking Luke's way. Cowan was a powerfully built man, slightly taller than Luke, with dark brown hair that hung to his shoulders, and a week's worth of stubble darkening his neck and jaw. His deep brown, almost black, eyes glared with hatred at Luke from under the battered, flat-crowned tan hat he wore.

"Well, if it ain't Texas Ranger Luke Caldwell," Cowan sneered, scowling. "I'd heard you were back in town, and damn, if I don't look out the window of Charlie's shop and see you struttin' down the street, big as life. You're finally gonna get what's comin' to you for jailin' my pa."

"Your pa went to jail for stealin' horses," Luke retorted. "I was only upholding the law."

"That don't matter none. I'm gonna whup you into the dirt for that."

"It takes a real brave man to attack one with a busted arm," Luke said. "It's not fair goin' after an *hombre* who can't defend himself. I'm not carryin' a gun, since until this arm heals up I can't even use one. That means if you pull your iron and plug me, you'll be hung for cold-blooded murder."

"That's your worry, not mine. And I dang for certain don't need a gun. I'm gonna take care of you once and for all, with my bare hands," Cowan said. He took a swing at Luke's chin. Luke sidestepped the blow easily, then sent a roundhouse left to the side of Cowan's nose, breaking it and smashing it sideways against his cheek. A gush of blood poured down Cowan's mouth and chin, then dripped onto his chest. He dropped to his knees, howling in pain.

"Hell, you done busted my nose, you damn bastard," he whimpered. "Son of a bitch."

"I told you it wasn't smart to pick on an *hombre* who can't defend himself," Luke answered, with a wicked grin. "Can't say I didn't warn you."

Before Cowan could answer, Deputy Marshal Steve Stephens hurried up, carrying a double-barreled, sawed-off shotgun.

"You just stay down, Russ," he ordered Cowan. "Luke, I saw the whole fracas from my office. Cowan started the trouble. You want me to press charges against the loco fool?"

"No, I think he's learned his lesson, Steve," Luke answered. "You might want to haul him down to Doc Patterson's, though, to get his nose shoved back in place."

"Hell, there's no need for that," Stephens answered. "I can handle that little chore myself. That honker will be straightened out in a jiffy. Stand up, Russ. Luke, hold my shotgun."

He passed the Greener to Luke, then, when Cowan hesitated, pulled him to his feet. He placed a hand on each side of Cowan's nose.

"This won't hurt much at all," he said, then pressed hard. Cartilage snapped when Stephens pushed the nose back in place. Cowan screeched in agony.

"Stop your whinin', Russ," Stephens ordered. "Mebbe Luke's right. I'd best take you down to

Doc's office, so he can bandage you up. But hell, your ugly mug looks better with that busted nose than it ever did before. Let's get goin'."

He took back his shotgun from Luke, and poked it into Cowan's back, shoving him along. Cowan spun, and attempted to wrest the Greener from the deputy's grasp. Stephens pulled the trigger of one barrel, sending a blast of closely bunched buckshot into Cowan's belly. His guts riddled, Cowan stumbled back, looking in disbelief at the scarlet spreading across his shirtfront.

"You, you done kilt me, Deputy. Damn you to Hell."

"You're gonna get there first," Stephens retorted. Cowan attempted to form an answer, but instead gasped for breath, fell to his knees, then rolled onto his side. He shuddered, and his body went slack.

"Plumb damn fool," Stephens muttered.

"You all right, Steve?" Luke asked.

"Yeah. Just my pride's hurt. I should've known better that to let Cowan get so close to my scattergun. Hell, even a rookie wouldn't have made that mistake."

"Nothin' you can do about it now," Luke told him. "Besides, someone was gonna have to kill Cowan, sooner or later. He was nothin' but trouble, just like his pa. He didn't give you any choice. Better it's him lyin' there in the dirt with a bellyful of buckshot, rather'n you."

"I reckon you're right about that," Stephens agreed. "Russ had it comin', that's for doggone certain. Better get him down to the undertaker's. Looks like Mort'll have a coffin to build."

Stephens chose two men from the crowd which had gathered.

"Morrissey, Garcia, you two haul what's left of Russ Cowan down to Engle's. The rest of you, break it up and get back to whatever you were doin'. There's nothin' more to see here.

"I guess I'd better wake up the marshal, to let him know what happened," Stephens said, once the body was removed and the crowd dispersed. "He's gonna be damn mad."

"What, about you pluggin' Cowan?" Luke said. "He'll have no call for that. You want me to go with you and help you explain exactly what happened?"

"No, that's not necessary," Stephens answered. "He won't be angry about me killin' Cowan, in fact, he'll most likely be plumb tickled. But, he's gonna be mad as a wet hen about me roustin' him out of bed, especially if the Widow Dawes spent the night at his house."

Luke raised an eyebrow.

"Bill Cherry and Clara Dawes? You've got to be kiddin' me. Heck, she's at least ten years older than Bill. I can't believe it."

"Eleven years older. But she's still a mighty fine lookin' woman," Stephens said. "She's had her cap set for Bill for quite a while now. I wouldn't be surprised if they get hitched before too much longer."

Luke shook his head.

"I never could've pictured that, not in my wildest imagination."

"When you stop by to see the marshal, you can bet he'll crow about the whole thing to you," Stephens answered. "Well, no use puttin' this off any longer. Where're you headed, Luke?"

"Over to Art's for a haircut, shave, and bath, then down to Doc Patterson's so he can look me over. Tell you what. I'll stop by the marshal's office on my way back."

"The coffee pot'll be on, like always," Stephens said. "See you later."

"Later, Steve."

I reckon Addie'll have a front page story for the next paper, Luke thought, as he resumed his walk. *And she'll want a first-hand account from me. Sure glad I know her well. Real well. Funny I never used to like newspaper editors. The ones I've known have always been tryin' to stir up trouble, or been in the pockets of the rich and powerful. Addie ain't like that at all. She tells the truth, and speaks her mind, and doesn't worry about where the chips might fall. Of course, I've never met another newspaper editor who looks as good as Addie, either, and for certain the only one I'd ever even think about sleepin' with. Yeah,*

I'm a lucky man all right. Got a job I enjoy, a wife who's the finest woman I've ever met, and a family who loves me. Lord, I thank You for all You've given me. I don't deserve any of Your gifts, but I'm mighty grateful for 'em.

He smiled to himself as he pulled open the door to the barber shop.

Chapter 5

Deputy Marshal George Dailey looked up from the wanted posters he was thumbing through when his boss, Sonora, Texas, Town Marshal Hank Brundage, stepped into the office.

"You're back from your last rounds of the day early, Marshal," he said.

"Yeah, I reckon I am," Brundage answered. "The town's even quieter than usual this evenin', if that's possible."

"Good. That means I should have a peaceful night too. The worst trouble I'll most likely have is breakin' up Widow Talbot's arguin' with Bob Mooney over his dog gettin' into her garden again, or mebbe bringin' in Ed Dwyer for drunk and disorderly. If he's no more blasted than usual, I'll let him sleep off his drunk in a cell, then turn him loose come mornin', as always."

"That *is* a busy night in Sonora," Brundage said, with a laugh.

"Yup. Boy howdy, it must be a lot easier for you bein' a small town marshal rather than a Texas Ranger, like you once was."

"It sure is," Brundage agreed. "The best part is being home with my wife just about every night, havin' home cooked meals, instead of bacon and beans most all the time, and sleeping on a soft mattress, with a roof over my head, rather'n on the hard ground under the sky."

"Do you ever miss bein' a Ranger, Marshal?"

"Sometimes, yeah. Not so much the work, as the freedom, and the friends I made. Of course, quite a few of them are dead now, killed by outlaw whites, Mexicans, or renegade Indians, or just plain gettin' sick and dyin' from dysentery or some other illness. I don't mind not havin' to watch my back every wakin' minute, that's for dang certain. Besides, when Sarah Jane agreed to marry me, I made the decision right there and then to quit the Rangers. She'd never have asked me to, but I knew that's what she wanted. More important, I didn't want to leave her a widow before she was thirty, or mebbe gettin' myself killed by a bushwhacker out in some God-forsaken canyon, never comin' home, and her never knowin' what happened to me."

"Was it hard givin' up the Rangers?"

"Not for Sarah, no sirree. She's the best thing that ever happened to me. Listen, George, I'm gonna get on outta here. Send for me if you need me."

"Sure thing, Marshal, but I most likely won't. This town's so quiet, it should be named 'Sonoring,' not Sonora. I'll see you in the mornin'. Good night. Tell Sarah Jane I said howdy."

"I'll do that. G'night, George."

Brundage knew it was feeding time at the Sonora Livery Stable, where he kept his horse, so rather than disturb the animal's meal, he decided to walk the short distance home. He paused on the boardwalk in front of his office just long enough to fill his pipe, touch a match to it, and take a long pull, then started for home. He whistled as he approached the tidy white cottage at the edge of town, where he'd settled down with Sarah Jane right after they'd married. He was looking forward to see what his wife had cooked for supper this evening, perhaps a roast beef, or even better, his favorite, chicken and dumplings. He caught a whiff of something delicious cooking when he stepped onto the front porch. Licking his lips in anticipation, he shoved open the front door. The minute he stepped inside, a gun barrel was shoved into the base of his spine.

"Just raise your hands over your head, Marshal," the man holding the gun ordered. "Don't make any sudden moves, or I'll blow your backbone clean out through your belly button. Do it!" he growled, when Brundage hesitated. "The hammer's cocked, and I've got a mighty itchy trigger finger, so this gun's liable to go off."

Realizing he didn't have a chance to reach his own six-gun before he got a chunk of lead in his back, Brundage complied, raising his hands shoulder high.

"That's better." The gunman slid Brundage's pistol out of its holster, and shoved it behind his own gun belt. "Truthfully, I'd like nothin' better than to plug you and be done with it, but Hutch has other plans for you, lawman. Get on into the kitchen."

He jabbed the barrel of his pistol deeper into Brundage's back, prodding him along. A lump of cold ice settled in the marshal's stomach, and fear gnawed at his guts, not for himself, but for his wife. What had the men who'd invaded his home done with Sarah Jane? His heart sank when he walked into the kitchen and his question was answered. Surrounded by three men pointing pistols at her, his wife was tied to a chair, her mouth gagged. She was as pale as death, the terror in her eyes evident. A fourth man stood between her and Brundage.

"Sarah Jane!" Brundage yelled. He ran toward his wife, only to be stopped in his tracks when the nearest man planted his foot solidly in the marshal's groin. Brundage moaned, clutched at his crotch, dropped to his knees and crumpled onto his side, curled up in agony.

"Williams, you . . . damn son of a . . . bitch," he managed to gasp out.

"Welcome home, Marshal," Hutchinson Williams said, with a sneer. "It's such a pleasure to visit with you again. I'd wager I'm the last person you expected to see. However, you really shouldn't cuss in front of any lady, especially not your wife."

Williams kicked Brundage in the belly, then used the toe of his boot to roll him onto his back.

"Listen to me, Marshal, and listen real good, 'cause I'm only gonna say this once. You're damn lucky I didn't tell Mace to go ahead and plug you in the back, if you tried anythin' stupid like you just did. You understand?"

Brundage nodded his head, spitting up blood. Apparently the kick to his stomach had burst open an artery, or perhaps a broken rib had punctured it.

"Good. Now, if you do everything I say, exactly as I say, then me and the boys just might, and I mean *might,* let the little lady live. You make one mistake, just one, and we'll cut her to ribbons, Comanche style. You'll watch her die, real slow. *Comprende?*"

Again, Brundage nodded his head.

"I knew you'd see it my way, Marshal. Mace, get him on his feet, but if he so much as twitches, put a bullet in him. Bryan, Jody, untie the woman. Take the gag out of her mouth, but if she starts to scream, shove it right back in there again. Slate, keep your gun on her, just in case she tries to run to her husband. If she does, shoot her down."

"And ruin all the fun we've got planned?" Slate Martin said. "That'd be a plumb shame, killin' a fine lookin' filly like this before we even got the chance to know her better."

"You heard me, Slate!" Williams snapped. "If she does try anythin', and you *don't* plug her, I'll put a bullet in *you,* then her. Understood?"

"Yeah, I reckon," Martin mumbled.

"Good."

Brundage was yanked to his feet, then slammed against a wall. Sarah Jane was untied, the gag removed from her mouth. She took in a deep breath, then started sobbing.

"Did any of these *hombres* hurt you, Sarah Jane?" Brundage asked. His wife regained her composure just long enough to answer him.

"No. No, they just frightened me so badly. But they haven't handled me too roughly."

She sniffled, then began crying again.

"There's no point in crying, Missy," Williams said. "As long as you cooperate with us, you'll be perfectly fine. If you do everythin' we say, why, we might even let your husband live."

"I . . . I don't believe you," Sarah Jane stammered.

"Whether you do or not don't make no never-mind to me," Williams answered. "But it might make a difference to the marshal over there. Show her, Mace."

Mason Williams drove a fist deep into Brundage's belly, jackknifing him, then followed the punch with one to his jaw, straightening him up and knocking him back against the wall. When Brundage began to sag, Mace grabbed him by the throat to hold him upright, then stuck the barrel of his gun into the marshal's mouth.

"You want me to blow his brains out right now, Hutch?" he asked.

"Not quite yet," Williams answered. To Sarah Jane he continued. "All I have to do is say the word, and my brother will blast your loving husband's brains clean out through the top of his skull. You wouldn't want that, would you?"

"No . . . no," Sarah Jane answered, with a sob.

"And you'll do everythin' we ask you to, right?"

"Yes. And you'll let Hank go?"

"I give you my word."

"Don't listen to him, Sarah Jane," Brundage told her. "He's a dirty, low-down liar. These men came here for one reason . . . to kill me. Nothin' you can say or do will stop them."

Sarah Jane trembled.

"Is what my husband says true, Mister?"

"Well, darlin', I'm afraid it is," Williams answered. "However, it's up to you exactly *how* he dies. If you do what we want, his death will be quick, and relatively painless. However, if you fight us, I promise you, your man will die very slowly, and only after a great deal of suffering. And, in that case, while he'll know he's dyin', he'll get to see you die before he does. Now, you sure wouldn't want to see him die like that, would you?"

"Don't listen to that monster, Sarah. He's insane," Brundage screamed. "What he'll do to you is even worse'n death."

"I . . . have to take the chance, Hank. If I can save you any suffering, any at all, then I have to try."

"You married a right smart woman, Marshal," Williams said. "Loyal, too. She knows how the game is played. Just mebbe, after you're dead, we'll take her along with us. Hell, she might even like that. Pardon my language, Mrs. Brundage."

"Williams, I swear, some day you'll pay for this," Brundage warned him. "I don't know how, or when, but, by God's justice, you'll pay."

"I doubt that," Williams answered. "Besides, you won't even know, since you'll already be dancin' with the Devil."

"C'mon, honey, no since puttin' this off any longer," he said to Sarah Jane. "We need to be gone before someone decides to stop by."

Sarah Jane shrank away when Williams undid the top button of her blouse. She slapped his face.

"Dammit, woman, you said you'd go along with me, and that's exactly what you're gonna do," Williams snarled. "I didn't realize you're quite the little spitfire. That's okay. I like a gal who plays rough."

He ripped open her blouse.

"My, my, I knew there had to be a nice package under all that gingham, but I never imagined how nice," Williams said, leering. When he attempted to kiss her, Sarah Jane clawed at his face, her fingernails ripping open his left eyeball and raking bloody tracks down both his cheeks. He screamed in pain and anger.

"You damned little bitch! You just half-blinded me!"

Williams punched her in the stomach. She doubled over in pain.

Brundage lunged at him, but only made two steps before Mace clubbed his pistol's barrel against the side of his head, cracking the marshal's skull and stunning him. Brundage stumbled backwards, hitting the wall, then bounced off, in another futile attempt to reach his wife. Mace then pulled a Bowie knife from its sheath on his belt, and plunged the heavy blade deep into Brundage's gut, burying it to the hilt. When he yanked the knife out, Brundage slumped back against the wall, then slid down to the floor, landing in a seated position, his hands clamped to his ripped open belly. Blood spread over his shirt and seeped between his fingers.

"Hank!" Sarah Jane screamed, in horror.

"Now see what you've done, woman," Williams snapped. "It's gonna take your husband a long time to die, and he's gonna see everythin' me and the boys do to you before he's gone. Then again, he might enjoy watchin'. Some men do."

He shoved Sarah Jane to the floor, unbuckled his gun belt and placed it on the table, then unbuttoned his denims. His skull fractured, life blood seeping away, Hank Brundage was helpless as Williams attacked his wife. He drifted in and out of consciousness, vaguely aware of his wife's screams. There was a short pause, when Williams finished his assault and one of the other men took his place. He heard that man yell and curse when Sarah Jane grabbed his hair and pulled out a large chunk. A sharp slap ripped the air, and Sarah Jane began pleading for mercy. The last sounds Brundage heard before death took him in its cold grasp were the screams of his wife, and the laughter of his killers.

Chapter 6

Luke laid his empty Winchester Model 1873 on the ground, then went into a crouch. He pulled his Colt SAA Army from its holster on his right hip in a smooth draw, and thumbed off six quick shots. Six tin cans jumped from the log on which they were perched, sixty feet distant. Luke thumbed the empties from the Peacemaker's chamber, reloaded, and thumbed off six more shots. Six more bullet punctured cans tumbled from the log.

"I reckon I'm back to just about good as new," Luke said to himself, as he reloaded the pistol. "It's about time, too."

He'd been home for just over a month now, and his arm had been out of the cast for two weeks. Despite how much he loved his family, and the time spent with them, he was getting restless. Luke had always had an itchy foot, and after two or three weeks at home, the need to be on the trail again, chasing lawbreakers, was almost overpowering. He hoped when he saw the doc next week he'd finally receive medical clearance saying he was fit for duty.

Luke chuckled softly when he slipped his six-gun back into its holster. When he'd first signed on with the Rangers, he'd been told he needed to practice a faster draw. Hell, he knew he wasn't the fastest gun puller in Texas, not by a long shot. As his comrades soon learned, accuracy was far more important than speed, anyway. The extra split second Luke took to make certain his bullet hit what he aimed at paid dividends. Quite a few quick-draw gun-fanners had found that out, when their shots missed, and Luke's first bullet put them in their graves.

Addie came out on the back porch when she saw Luke approaching. Scout was with her. He came bounding up to Luke, who reached down and scratched the dog's ears.

"I was just coming to get you, Luke," she called. "I'm done with the paper for today. Why don't you sit out here, and I'll bring you some lemonade?"

"That sure sounds good, honey. *Gracias.* C'mon, Scout."

Luke settled in one of the porch rockers. He unbuttoned his shirt to allow the late afternoon sun to soothe his almost healed belly wound. Scout curled up and lay down at Luke's feet. Luke had barely leaned back in his chair when Addie returned, carrying two glasses of lemonade. She handed one to Luke, then sat in the chair alongside his. She sipped at her glass, while Luke took a large swallow, then sighed in satisfaction.

"Boy howdy, this sure tastes good," he said.

"And to think you had to talk me into buyin' that icebox. I don't know how we ever got along without it."

"With great difficulty, that's how," Addie answered. She took another sip of her lemonade.

"I heard you practicing your shooting again, Luke. How did it go?"

"Real well. My aim's as good as it ever was, and I can get my six-gun out of its holster just about as fast as I ever could."

"Which means you'll be leaving shortly."

"I don't know about that quite yet. I have to wait and see what Doc Patterson says. I can't go back on duty without his say-so."

"But you're ready to. I can tell. You've been restless for the past week, and I've caught you gazing at the horizon, more than once."

"I have to admit it," Luke conceded. "I love you and the kids more'n anythin' else in this world, but there's somethin' inside me that has to keep me on the move. I know it must hurt you, and the kids, when I ride off. I just can't help it. Mebbe someday, when I get too old to chase renegades . . ."

Luke's voice trailed off.

"I can't picture that day ever coming, at least not for many years," Addie said. "Wanderlust is in your blood. The need to bring lawbreakers to justice is in it, too. I long ago accepted you'll be gone for weeks, or months, at a time. Besides, sometimes I do get tired of having you underfoot, you know."

"Oh, you do, do you?"

"I certainly do. Not that I wouldn't mind having you around a little more often."

"What was that you said was in my blood. Wander—?"

"Wanderlust."

"That's not the only kind of lust that's in my blood," Luke said. He leaned over and kissed Addie's cheek.

"You're incorrigible, cowboy. I hope you know that," Addie said, with a smile.

"If that means I want to make love to you all the time, I confess that I'm guilty," Luke said. "I'll just have to throw myself on the mercy of the court." He began to kiss Addie again, but stopped when Scout lifted his head, growled softly, then raced off the porch and down the alley alongside the building.

"I wonder what Scout heard," Addie said.

"He probably smelled a cat, or some kind of rodent," Luke answered. "That wasn't his warning growl sayin' someone was comin'."

"Perhaps you should go check, just to be certain."

"Mebbe you're right."

Luke pushed himself up from his chair. Just as he got to his feet, four people came around the corner of the building, Junction Town

Marshal Bill Cherry, Reverend Otis Campbell of the Sonora Christian Community Church, along with his wife, Cordelia, and Harry Cole, the telegrapher from the local Western Union office. Scout ran ahead of them and back onto the porch. Luke's heart skipped a beat. Those four individuals coming for an unannounced visit could only mean one thing, something was drastically wrong. The somber expressions on their faces confirmed it. When a look of shock crossed Cordelia Campbell's face, and she placed a hand to her mouth in surprise, Luke remembered his shirt was still open. His face flushed crimson as he hastily buttoned the garment.

"I'm plumb sorry, Mrs. Campbell," he apologized. "We weren't expectin' anyone to come callin' this afternoon."

"That's quite all right, Luke," Reverend Campbell assured him. "This visit wasn't planned, so there's no need to apologize that you and Adeline weren't prepared for company. I'm afraid it's also a hard one to make. Would you mind if we went inside?"

"No, not at all," Addie answered. "We'll go into the living room. Would you like me to brew some coffee?"

"Perhaps later," Marshal Cherry said. "Luke, Addie, I'm afraid we've got some bad news for you. Real bad. That's why Harry got me, and I got the Reverend and his missus, to come with him. No, it's not any of your kids," he continued. "They're still in school, safe and sound."

"Marshal, please, come inside where we'll be more comfortable," Addie said. "Also, where no one might accidentally overhear, or perhaps even eavesdrop, on our conversation."

She opened the door, and everyone trooped into the living room. Once all were seated, Luke spoke up.

"All right, Marshal, there's no point keepin' me 'n Addie waitin'. What've you got to tell us?"

"Okay, Luke, here it is. Hank Brundage, your brother-in-law, is dead. He was murdered. As far as your sister, well, the only information that was sent from Sonora says she's in bad shape."

Addie gasped. Luke swallowed hard.

"Hank's been murdered?" he said. "And my sister's hurt? Who did it?"

"Apparently the law in Sonora hasn't figured that out yet," Cherry answered. "Harry, give Luke that wire."

Cole handed Luke a yellow flimsy, which was addressed to Marshal Cherry.

Advise L. Caldwell Msl Brundage killed STOP His sister badly wounded STOP Assailants unknown STOP Need him Sonora asap STOP Act Mshl G Dailey STOP

After reading the telegram, Luke crumpled the paper in his fist. His eyes welled with tears.

"Harry, this message is dated eight days ago. What took it so dang long to arrive?"

"Apparently no one in Sonora knew you were back home, so it was sent to the Adjutant General's Office in Austin, to be forwarded to you at your company's camp. They sent it to Major Jones, who sent a reply back to Austin, who then attempted to send a reply back to Sonora. But a wicked storm had downed a whole section of line, so the reply didn't reach Sonora until after repairs were made. That's the reason for the delay."

"Luke, you have to go to your sister," Addie said. "That is, as long as you feel up to the trip."

"You beat me to it," Luke answered. "And you can be darn certain I'm up to the trip. Weren't we just talking about that?"

"Yes, but you said you had to wait until Doctor Patterson gave you clearance to return to duty," Addie reminded him.

"That just changed," Luke answered. "It's about sixty miles to Sonora, more or less. If I get started right now, I can be there late tomorrow afternoon or early evening. I'll visit with Sarah Jane, get all the information the local law has, then get on the trail of whoever did this. I won't be back until I find them, and they're behind bars, waitin' to be hung . . . or dead, with my bullets in 'em."

"That will mean ridin' all night, then all day tomorrow. You haven't been in the saddle for over a month, Luke. You can't possibly make the ride that quick," Cherry objected.

"I've done it before, sometimes in pretty bad shape," Luke answered. "I won't have to ride all night in any event. Both my horses have had plenty of rest, so they're ready for a long run. I'll ride until about midnight or early morning, stop and grab a few hours shut-eye, then start out again at first light. Takin' both horses means I can switch them out, so neither one'll get overworked. Bill, you of all people should know I'd never abuse a horse, or run one into the ground."

"Yeah, you always have said the dumbest horse is smarter than most people," Cherry conceded.

"Honey, if you're going to start, you shouldn't waste any time," Addie said. "I'll put some food together for you to take along, and your spare clothes, while you get your horses ready and gather your gear."

"My husband and I will stay with you for a while, if you'd like, Addie," Cordelia offered.

"I would appreciate that, as long as you agree to stay to supper," Addie answered. "The same goes for you, Marshal, and for you, Harry."

"We'd be delighted to have supper with you," Cordelia answered. "Plus I'm certain you'll appreciate our company."

"I've got to be home for supper," Cherry answered. "My wife has her sewing circle meeting tonight, so I have to watch the kids. But I'm obliged for the offer."

"I'd love to take you up on the invitation, but I need to get back to my office," Cole said. "Dan Tulley, the night operator, is out sick, so I have to cover for him. In fact, I'd better get movin'."

"Hold on just a minute before you leave, Harry," Luke said. "You got a paper and pencil?"

"Of course."

Cole fished a stub of pencil and a telegram form out of his shirt pocket. He handed those to Luke.

"Here ya go."

"*Gracias*."

Luke hastily scrawled out a message, then handed it to the telegrapher.

"Send that off to the Adjutant General's office. Also send a copy to the town where the wire from Major Jones came. He'll have left instructions where he'll be at, so we'll be certain the message gets through by sending it to both places. It explains what happened, and that I'm on my way to Sonora."

"It'll go out right now, soon as I get back to the office," Cole promised. "I'm sure sorry about your brother-in-law and sister, Luke. Good luck, and stay safe."

"*Gracias*, Harry."

"I'll go with you, Harry," Cherry said. "I have to swing by my office before I go home, anyway.

Luke, my sympathies. Tell Sarah Jane I said howdy, and that I'm sorry for her loss. And when you find whoever did this, put an extra bullet in 'em for me."

"My cartridge belt doesn't hold near enough as many slugs as I'd like to put in those sons of . . . guns," Luke answered, changing his words in the nick of time when he remembered the ladies, and preacher, present. "I'll make certain a couple of 'em have your name on 'em, Bill."

"Make sure they do, Luke. *Vaya con Dios.*"

"*Adios.*"

"Luke, do you mind if I come along while you prepare your horses?" Reverend Campbell asked.

"Not at all, Reverend, in fact, I'd be obliged."

"Thank you, Luke."

While Addie and Cordelia went inside the house, Luke and the reverend headed for the barn. Pete and RePete were in their corral, lying on their sides and soaking up the sun. When Luke whistled, the paints scrambled to their feet, shook themselves off, and trotted over to the fence. Luke took two pieces of molasses candy from his vest pocket, gave one to each horse, and opened the gate.

"You two boys ready to head out?" he said to the horses. "You've been hangin' around gettin' fat and lazy long enough. It's high time we hit the trail again."

The horses trotted inside the barn and into their

stalls. Luke poured a full measure of grain into their feed bins, along with a flake of hay for each. After filling their buckets with water, Luke got a currycomb and began grooming Pete.

"Luke, you don't mind my speaking while you work on your horses, do you?" Campbell asked.

"No, not at all," Luke answered. "Why? Do you have anythin' in particular on your mind?"

"As a matter of fact, I do."

"Then speak your piece."

"All right. Luke, I know that as a lawman, you have a strong sense of duty, one that is no doubt compelling you to find the man or men who committed this horrible crime. You also undoubtedly desire to see justice done, and those responsible pay for their evil actions. However, I have to ask you this, and I hope you'll give me an honest answer. Are you going after the perpetrators to see justice done, or are you intent on seeking vengeance? If it's the latter, then I would urge you to reconsider your decision, and let another member of the Rangers, or the county sheriff, handle the case, while you care for your sister. She's going to need you with her, perhaps for quite some time. I also have to wonder if this case is too personal for you."

Luke hesitated before replying.

"Reverend, you asked for an honest answer, and I'm goin' to give you one. You're right about one thing, this is dang personal for me. The truth is, I'm not certain which is the stronger reason I'm goin' after those *hombres*. In my mind, yes, I want to track down whoever is responsible for my brother-in-law Hank's murder, and the attack on my sister, and see them face a judge and jury. However, the desire to get revenge on those men is gnawin' at my guts like a cancer. I can't say for certain that, when I do catch up with 'em, I won't just gun 'em down like the rabid dogs they are. So I guess what I'm sayin' is, I won't know what I'll do until I actually confront those bastards. Pardon my language."

"Under the circumstances, your language is understandable, Luke, so you're forgiven for it. However, I would like to point out to you, that if you do shoot down those men without giving them the opportunity to surrender, then you would also be a murderer, and little better than them. You should also remember that 'Vengeance is Mine, sayeth the Lord.'"

"Not by my lights, Reverend. I'd be upholding the law, and ridding the world of some no-good scum. And I'd be the Lord's right hand in meting out His vengeance. Sometimes even He needs a little help."

"Need I remind you even the worst criminal has the right to a fair trial, Luke? I truly hope you haven't forgotten that."

"Of course you don't. I'll tell you what, Reverend. I'll promise to do my level best to bring those men back alive, since I'd rather see 'em sweat before they stretch a rope, myself. However, if they put up the least bit of fight, at all, they'll die on the spot. You can bet your hat on that."

"That would be a pretty safe bet, since I never wear a hat," Campbell answered, with a chuckle. "However, I appreciate your candor. I'll pray that, when the time comes, you make the right decision."

"I'm obliged. Prayers are somethin' I can always use, Reverend," Luke answered. "Thank you."

He patted Pete's neck.

"I'm done curryin' you, Pete," he told the horse. "Finish chowin' down while I work on your brother."

After grooming RePete and checking his shoes, Luke got his saddle blanket, saddle and saddlebags, and bridles from their peg on the wall. He saddled and bridled Pete, then hung RePete's bridle from his saddle horn, along with his lariat and canteen. Lastly, he attached a long lead rope to RePete's halter, and tied it loosely around the gelding's neck.

"We'll be travelin' fast and hard, so you fellas won't have to carry a pack saddle this trip," he said, as he led the paints out of the barn. Addie and Mrs. Campbell were waiting on the porch. Luke dropped his horses' reins, ground hitching them.

"You two stand hitched," he ordered. "I've just got to gather a few things."

"I've got your spare clothes, and some sandwiches for you, Luke," Addie said. "Is there anything else I can help you with?"

Luke shook his head.

"I don't think so. I've only got to get my rifle, and some extra ammunition, then I'll be ready to travel. I already filled my canteen from the barn pump."

He went inside, and emerged a few minutes later carrying his Winchester and two boxes of shells. He shoved the rifle in its saddle scabbard, and put the ammunition in his saddlebags, along with the food and spare clothing Addie handed him.

"Luke, would you mind if I lay hands on you, and offer a prayer, before you leave?" Campbell asked.

"Of course not, Reverend."

The minister put his hands on Luke's shoulders. Luke removed his hat, and both bowed their heads.

"Lord, we beseech Thee, to keep Thy servant, Luke Caldwell, safe on his quest to find the evildoers who assaulted his sister, Sarah Jane Brundage, and murdered her husband, Hank. We also ask that You lead him to the men responsible, and give him the courage and strength to bring them to justice. In addition, we ask Your eternal rest for Hank Brundage, and a rapid and full recovery for Sarah Jane. We ask You to grant our requests in the name of Your Son, Our Savior, Jesus Christ. Amen."

"Amen. *Muchas gracias*, Reverend."

Luke turned to Addie. He took her in his arms for a long, lingering kiss.

"Don't worry about me. I'll be just fine," he tried to reassure her. "Tell the kids I'm sorry I had to leave without sayin' good-bye. Tell 'em I love 'em, and give 'em a kiss and hug for me."

"Of course, Luke." Addie kissed him again. "You take care of yourself. Give Sarah Jane my love, and tell her if she needs anything, anything at all, to send me a message. If she'd like to come stay with me and the children for a while, once she feels well enough, she's more than welcome."

"I'll let her know," Luke said. "Well, I'd best get movin' if I'm gonna make Sonora before dark tomorrow."

He climbed into his saddle, then leaned down to give Addie one final kiss.

"*Adios*, honey. I'll wire you soon as I reach Sonora, and find out how Sarah Jane's doin'."

He put Pete into a walk, with RePete trailing behind. Five minutes later, he was out of Addie's sight. After a quarter mile, once the horses were warmed up, Luke heeled Pete into a mile eating lope, a gait that would cover plenty of ground, without wearing the horses out. Alternating between the lope, walk, and trot, switching horses every few hours, Luke would reach Sonora before dusk the next night.

Chapter 7

Luke arrived in Sonora just after five the next afternoon. He stopped at the trough in the town square to allow his tired horses a short drink, then rode straight to the town marshal's office.

"I'll get you boys settled in at the livery stable as soon as I can," Luke promised his horses, as he dismounted, and looped their reins over the hitch rail. He gave each a piece of molasses candy, then ducked under the rail and went inside the office. Acting Marshal George Dailey was at his desk, sorting through wanted posters. He looked up when Luke stepped through the door.

"Howdy. Can I help you, Mister?" he asked.

"Evenin', Marshal. Yeah, you sure can help me. I'm Texas Ranger Lieutenant Luke Caldwell, come to see my sister. After that, I want you to tell me everythin' you know about the men who killed her husband and I guess just about killed her, too, so I can get on their trail, unless you've already caught 'em."

"I'm real glad to see you, Lieutenant," Dailey said, as he stood up and extended his hand, which Luke shook. "No, whoever's responsible is still on the loose. Honestly, I don't have anythin' much to go on. I'm sure sorry about what happened to your sister and brother-in-law. I'm also sorry

137

about the delay in the message reaching you. You made dang good time, considerin'."

"I started out yesterday, soon as I received the wire," Luke said. "I've got a couple of real good horses, so I only had to stop and rest 'em for a couple of hours. There's no need to apologize about the telegram being sent to the wrong place. That wasn't your fault. And the name's Luke. But I need to ask you, straight out, since you haven't said, how is my sister doin'?"

"Long as you call me George. Truthfully, I'd rather let Doc Clayton explain Sarah Jane's condition to you." Dailey glanced at the Regulator clock on the wall behind his desk. "Tell you what. Zack Eakins, my night deputy, should be along any minute. This place can handle itself until he gets here. Your sister's still at the doc's. We'll head over there now. After you visit with her, we can have supper at the Sonora Station Café, and talk things over while we eat. I'd imagine you're pretty damn hungry. Joe Dawkins, who owns the place, serves up some mighty fine grub."

"I doggone sure can choke down a bite or two, that's for damn certain," Luke answered.

"Then let's go."

Dailey took his hat from a peg on the wall, and jammed it on his head.

"The doc's is only about four blocks down," he said, as they left the office. "I have to warn you, I don't know how your sister will react when she sees you. She hasn't said a word since that day. She's been in and out of consciousness until just three days ago, so she couldn't even make Hank's funeral." Dailey paused, swallowed hard, sighed, then continued. "What happened to Hank and Sarah Jane has hit this whole town hard. Everybody loved both of 'em. We're all pullin' for Sarah Jane. For me, Hank wasn't just my boss, but a good friend. He taught me pretty much everything I know about law work. Funny thing is, the night he got killed, me'n him were talkin' about what a quiet town Sonora is. He told me how much easier it was bein' a town marshal than a Texas Ranger. Just goes to show you never know. Did you and Hank ever ride together, when he was with the Rangers?"

"We sure did," Luke answered. "We were ridin' pards for a little more'n two years. In fact, that's how he met my sister, when he came home with me on leave. Next thing I knew, he up and quit the Rangers, married Sarah Jane, and took the marshal's job here in Sonora. He was a real decent *hombre*, and one of the best lawmen I've ever met. He was Sarah Jane's first and only love. I don't know how she'll get along without him. I know I'm sure gonna miss him."

"I understand," Dailey answered. "Well, here's Doc Clayton's."

Dailey opened the gate of a low rock wall, which led to a small, whitewashed adobe house.

Colorful flowers bloomed in large clay pots on either side of the front door. When Dailey knocked, a woman in her middle fifties, slightly plump, with gray hair and sparkling blue eyes, answered.

"Why, good evening, Marshal," she said. "We weren't expecting you to drop by tonight."

"Evenin', Mrs. Clayton," Dailey answered. "This here's Lieutenant Luke Caldwell, of the Texas Rangers. He's Miz Brundage's brother."

"Evenin', ma'am," Luke said. "I'm sorry to trouble you this late, and without any warnin'."

"Pish-tosh. It's no bother at all. I'm certain your sister will be pleased to see you. Come right in. I'll fetch the doctor."

"Thank you, ma'am," Luke said. He and Dailey removed their hats and stepped into a short hallway. Mrs. Clayton indicated a parlor to the right.

"You gentlemen, please, wait in here and make yourselves comfortable while I get my husband. I'll only be a moment."

"That's Clarissa Clayton," Dailey explained, once she was gone. "She's the doc's wife and also his nurse. A kinder woman you'll never meet."

"She seems like that," Luke agreed. "Hope she hurries right back. I'm really anxious to see Sarah Jane."

"She will," Dailey assured him.

A few moments later, Mrs. Clayton returned, accompanied by a man of about her age, who was dressed in a neatly pressed white shirt and black trousers. He was a bit taller than average, with brown hair, gray at the temples, and a carefully trimmed spade beard. His sharp brown eyes peered from behind a pair of pince-nez spectacles, which were perched on the tip of his nose.

"Ranger Caldwell, this is my husband, Dr. William Clayton," she said. "William, this is Sarah Jane's brother, Ranger Lieutenant Luke Caldwell."

"I'm pleased to meet you, Ranger Caldwell, although of course I wish it were under happier circumstances," Clayton said, as they shook hands. "If you have no objections, I'd like to take a moment to explain your sister's condition before I bring you to see her."

"No, not at all," Luke said.

"Very well. Sarah Jane suffered a severe beating at the hands of the monsters who committed this foul deed. Amazingly, she has no broken bones, which can only be a miracle by the grace of God. However, she does have severe swelling, abrasions and contusions . . ."

"Abrasions and contusions?"

"Scrapes and bruises, along with scratches and some long cuts. Again, just like her having no broken bones, miraculously Sarah Jane's injuries required no stitches. Both her eyes were blackened and swollen shut. The swelling around her eyes has gone down sufficiently so she is now able to see.

"I am not particularly worried about her external injuries. However, your sister was raped, violently raped, and from what I can tell, which is educated speculation on my part, by more than one man. While the physical injuries will, in time, heal, I am very concerned about her mental state. She's had a major trauma. As I'm certain, Deputy—I mean Marshal—Dailey has probably told you, she hasn't spoken a single word since the day everything happened. I'm hoping seeing you will help trigger some response. I do have to advise you, while she is awake, she has been completely incommunicative since regaining consciousness. Part of that can be attributed to the laudanum I've had her on, to ease her pain and keep her resting, but much of it I'm afraid is due to the shock of what she has been through. I merely wanted you to know what to expect when you walk into her room. If you're ready, I'll take you to her right now."

"I'm more'n ready, Doc," Luke answered. "Lead the way."

Although Luke thought he had steeled himself against showing any sign of distress when he first saw his sister, he had to stifle a gasp when he walked into her room. Sarah Jane was sitting in a chair alongside her bed, staring out the window. A thick bandage covered her left ear, another held her broken nose in place. Her eyes were blackened, her face swollen and bruised. Not wanting to startle her, Luke spoke her name softly.

"Sarah Jane."

She turned and looked at him, showing no sign of recognition.

"Sarah Jane. It's me, Luke. Your brother."

"Luke?" Sarah Jane's eyes widened. She stood up, and broke down sobbing. Luke put his arms around her in a tight hug.

"It's all right, Sis. Go ahead and cry, much as you need to," he said. "I'm here now."

Luke held his sister until her sobbing subsided.

"Why don't you lie back down? I'll sit alongside you," he suggested.

"Your brother is right. You really should lie down again, Mrs. Brundage. You still need plenty of rest. It's also a good sign to hear you speak again," Doctor Clayton added. "I was afraid your larynx, that is, your voice box, might have been damaged, or perhaps you'd had a concussion which affected the area of your brain which controls speech."

"All . . . all right. Doctor. I apologize I haven't spoken sooner. I've just been . . . so afraid."

"That's understandable," Clayton answered.

"You need to recover at your own pace. If you try to rush things, it could cause a setback."

Sarah Jane got back into bed. She plumped her pillow so she could sit up, then pulled the covers over her legs. Luke sat in the ladder back chair next to her.

"First, I want to say how sorry I am about you having Hank taken from you. I'm gonna miss him almost as much as you will, since we were friends and ridin' pards. I also want to say I'm sorry I didn't get here sooner, but there was a mix-up between Headquarters, my company's location, and where I was, plus a problem with Western Union's lines. I just received the message yesterday, and lit right out. I got here as quick as I could."

"I understand, Luke. I'm just so glad you're here now."

"I know this is going to sound like a dumb question, but how are you feeling, Sis?"

"Honestly, I can't say. My emotions are all mixed up. I get angry, then depressed, then feel guilty, then sometimes think what happened was just an awful nightmare that I'll wake up from, and Hank will be with me. My body hurts, but that's nothing compared to the other things those men did to me. Luke, I watched them kill Hank, right in front of me. I did everything they asked me to do, and the leader said they'd spare Hank's life if I did, but they killed him anyway. He told me they would, just before he was murdered. When he tried to stop them from, from . . ."

Sarah Jane broke down, sobbing.

"It's okay, Sis," Luke said. "You don't have to say any more, if it's too hard on you."

"No. No, I have to get through this," Sarah Jane answered. She took a deep breath, then continued. "When the leader of those horrible men tore open my dress, then punched me, Hank tried to stop him, even though one of the other men held a gun on him. That man clubbed his gun over Hank's head, then stabbed him. I'm not . . . certain how long Hank lived, but I know . . . it was long enough for him to see . . . some of what those men did to me. Oh, I feel so *dirty!*"

She broke down crying once again.

"What happened wasn't your fault, Sis," Luke said. "Hank knows that, even though he's gone, and I know it. As soon as I'm certain you're well enough I can leave you, and I get all the information about those men I can, I'll be on their trail. I won't quit chasing them until they're all behind bars, waiting to be hung, or dead, filled with lead from my gun. You have my word on it."

"That still won't bring Hank back, or erase the images from that night. Those are seared inside my head as if they'd been branded onto my brain."

"I know, Sis. But those men have to be punished. It's my duty as a lawman to bring them in. And as your brother, it's a blood vow."

Sarah Jane fell back onto her pillow. She lay motionless, staring up at the ceiling.

"Sis?"

Luke received no response.

"Sis?" he repeated.

"Oh, go away and just leave me be," she said, her voice bitter. "Just get out of here, all of you."

"Are you certain?" Luke asked.

"Absolutely."

"All right, Sis, if that's what you want. I'll be back to see you in the morning. If you need me before then, just send word to the hotel, and I'll be back faster'n a roadrunner chasin' a lizard."

"I just want my husband back. I want things to be the way they were."

"I know, Sis."

"Ranger Caldwell, I believe this is enough time for this evening," Clayton said. "It wouldn't do for your sister to become so overwrought she has a setback. Also, you appear as if you could use a good night's sleep yourself. I know it must have been a difficult two days for you, first receiving the tragic news, then a hard ride here."

"I can't argue with you about that," Luke admitted.

"William, I think it would be best if all of you left Mrs. Brundage alone for a while," Mrs.

146

Clayton spoke up. "Sometimes, a woman just needs to be alone with another woman. I'll stay with her until she falls back to sleep."

"That's good advice, darling," Clayton agreed.

"Yeah, and I need to get all the information Marshal Dailey has for me before I turn in," Luke said. "Sarah Jane, you get some more rest, so you can recover, quick as you can. I'll see you in the mornin'."

He leaned over and kissed her cheek.

"Thank you, Luke," she whispered. "I truly am glad you're here. I really am. It's just . . ."

"Hush, child. Not another word," Mrs. Clayton ordered. "I'll be right back with some tea and chicken soup. Won't that be lovely? You do need to take more nourishment, so you can regain your strength."

"Yes, that will be all right," Sarah Jane answered.

"Excellent. William, gentlemen, shoo."

"You heard my wife," Clayton said, with a soft chuckle. "I may be the physician, but she issues the orders."

A short time later, Pete and RePete were settled in comfortable stalls at the livery stable, munching on hay after having a full measure of grain. Satisfied his horses would be well cared for, Luke joined Marshal Dailey at the Sonora Station Café. Both men were now working on their suppers of thick steaks, boiled potatoes, and pinto beans, with plenty of hot, black coffee.

"Okay, George, tell me everything you know about my brother-in-law's murder and sister's rape," Luke said.

"I will, but unfortunately, it'll be a pretty short story," Dailey answered. "There's not much to go on."

"No witnesses?"

Dailey shook his head.

"Nary a one. The crime wasn't discovered until the next morning. When Hank didn't show up for work, I went to his house looking for him. That's when I discovered him dead, and Sarah Jane badly beaten and still unconscious. First thing I did was get the doc for her, then I started searching for clues. I found where the men responsible had hidden their horses, then followed their tracks to the road. Five horses, so I'm assuming five men were involved. Once they reached the road, the hoof prints got mixed in with all the others, so it was impossible to tell which way they headed. They could have gone anywhere. I combed through the house, but couldn't find anything there, either. As your sister told you, Hank had his skull cracked open by a gun barrel, then he was gutted with a knife, so there were no bullets lodged in any of the walls or furniture, nor any shell casings. That's another reason none of the townsfolk heard anything.

Since it seems no one fired a gun, there were no gunshots to give those *hombres* away. Whoever did this planned it damn well. The only clue we have, and it's a mighty slim one, was a hank of hair your sister still had clutched in her hand. She must have yanked it out while tryin' to fight off one of the bastards who raped her. I can tell you I made certain no one besides myself has been in the house since that day. I figured you'd want to go through the place once you arrived."

"You're damn right I do," Luke said. "Soon as we've finished with supper you can take me over there."

"I could, but it'd probably be better to wait until mornin'," Dailey answered. "The light'll be stronger, so that will give you a better chance to find somethin' I might've missed. I'm only a small town lawman, more used to breakin' up fistfights or jailin' drunks than dealing with murderers. You're a Ranger, which means you just might find somethin' I overlooked. Tell you what. Soon as we finish supper, we'll head on over to my office. I'll let you read my report, plus I'll show you the hair we found in Sarah Jane's hand. After that, if you want, we can stop by the Copper Canyon Saloon for some drinks before you turn in. Tomorrow, soon as it's light enough, we can go over to your sister's house."

"That sounds like as good a plan as any," Luke agreed. "After I go through the house, I'll head to the doc's and visit my sister again. With any luck, she'll be ready to talk more about what happened, and mebbe give us some descriptions of those sons of bitches."

Luke and Dailey finished their meal, lingered over final cups of coffee and cigarettes, then went to the marshal's office. Dailey waved Luke to a seat.

"Have a chair, Luke," he said. "I've got the report and hair right here in my desk. You want a smoke?"

"I've got the makin's, but thanks."

After he and Luke rolled and lit quirlies, Dailey opened the desk's center drawer, took out two sheets of paper, and passed those to Luke, who quickly read the brief report, then handed it back to Dailey.

"You weren't lyin', George," he said. "There's not a damn thing in here than will help me track down those *hombres*. How about that piece of hair you found in my sister's hand?"

"I've got it right here."

Dailey handed Luke a fairly long, thick hank of strawberry blond hair.

"That's it. Looks like the *hombre* wore his hair pretty long."

"So one of the bastards I'm lookin' for has reddish blond, shoulder length or thereabouts hair," Luke muttered. "That narrows it down to only a few thousand men in Texas."

"Only one of which'll be missin' a chunk of hair," Dailey said.

"So all I need to do is ask every man in the state with this color hair to take off his hat and let me see if he's got a missin' piece," Luke said. "That should only take me forty or fifty years. By the time I'm done, most of 'em will have turned gray, so I won't be able to make a match anyway."

"Or gone bald," Dailey added, with a bitter laugh. "Luke, you can't say I didn't warn you I wouldn't be much help."

"And you damn sure weren't lyin'," Luke answered. "You mind if I keep this hair?"

"Not at all," Dailey said. "Long as you promise, once you catch up with the *hombre* who owns it, you take the rest of his scalp for me. I've got a better idea. Lemme separate this hair into two pieces. That way, if the *hombre* it belongs to is fool enough to show back here, I'll have enough left I can match it to the bastard."

"It's a deal, George. Now, I dunno about you, but I'm damn sure ready for those drinks."

"Same here," Dailey said. "The Copper Canyon's only a few doors down from here, so we'll be bellyin' up to the bar in no time. Let's go."

"Luke, I'll buy the drinks," Dailey said, once they were standing at the long bar inside the Copper Canyon. "What'll you have?"

"Whiskey," Luke answered.

"Same as I'm havin'."

Dailey signaled to the nearest bartender, who hurried over.

"Evenin', Marshal," the man said. He was in his late thirties, a bit on the pudgy side, with dark brown hair, parted down the middle and carefully pomaded in place, brown eyes, and an impressive handlebar moustache. He wore a clean, pressed and starched white shirt, its sleeves held in place by black garters, and black trousers. A freshly laundered white apron protected his clothing.

"Evenin', Harley," Dailey answered. "This here's Texas Ranger Lieutenant Luke Caldwell. He's Sarah Jane Brundage's brother. He'll only be in town for a day or two, just long enough to visit with his sister, try'n figure out who might've been behind the attack on her, and the marshal's murder, then light out after 'em. Luke, Harley Martin. He owns this here saloon."

Martin extended his hand, which Luke shook.

"I'm pleased to meet you, Lieutenant," he said. "I'm plumb sorry about what happened to your sister, and of course the killin' of your brother-in-law. I sure hope you can track down the sons of bitches responsible. Hank was a real fine *hombre*, and your sister, well, your sister's one of the most decent women I've ever met. She had a kind word to say about everyone, and always had a smile on her face. She didn't have any airs about her, neither. She'd say howdy to any of my percentage gals if she met one on the street, just as soon as she would one of the society ladies. No sir, the Good Lord don't make 'em any better than Sarah Jane."

"I appreciate your kind words, Harley. Call me Luke. You mind if I ask you a few questions?"

"Not at all, but let me get your drinks first. What're you havin'?"

"We're havin' rye," Dailey answered. "None of your cheap rot-gut, either. Bring us a bottle of Old Overholt. You can put it on my tab."

"Which, if you ever paid up, would make me a rich man, George," Martin said, with a laugh. "Hold on just one minute."

Martin rummaged under the bar, until he came up with an unopened bottle of the requested brand, and two glasses, which he placed in front of Luke and the marshal. He uncorked the bottle and filled both glasses three quarters full.

"There you are, gentlemen," he said. "Enjoy."

"Oh, we will," Dailey said. He and Luke downed their drinks in one swallow, then Dailey refilled their glasses.

"I'd imagine that cut the rest of the trail dust from your gullet, Luke," he said.

"It did just that," Luke answered. He took another sip from his glass. "This here's mighty fine red-eye."

"It's a good sippin' whiskey," Martin said. "Smooth, isn't it?"

"That it is," Luke agreed.

"You said you had some questions for me, Luke? You mind asking them now, so I can get back to my other customers. I hate to put too much work on my assistants."

"Not at all," Luke said. "Just give me a minute to build a smoke."

He took his sack of Bull Durham, packet of papers, and the small, corked bottle which contained his matches from his vest pocket, and rolled a cigarette. He took a lucifer from the bottle, scratched it to life on the sole of his boot, then touched it to the quirly. He took a deep drag on his smoke, then exhaled a ring of blue smoke toward the ceiling.

"I'm ready, Harley. These won't take long."

"Go ahead."

"The first one is, were there any strangers drinkin' in here anytime during, let's say, the week before Hank Brundage was murdered?"

"No, not that I recollect . . . and I recollect everyone who comes into my place."

"I can tell you, no one in town saw anyone new ride in or out before Hank was murdered," Dailey added. "He or she would've known if anyone had, and let me'n the other deputies know. Whoever killed Hank laid real low, and made certain they weren't spotted."

"So none of your assistants noticed anyone out of place, Harley?"

"Nope," Martin answered.

"What about any of your gals, Harley?" Luke pressed. "There any chance one of 'em might've met someone on the street, and decided to provide a little private entertainment?"

"I suppose it's possible, but I doubt it. One of the town busybodies would have been certain to notice, and the news would've been all over town in no time. You know how fast word spreads in a small town like Sonora."

"I can tell you ain't nobody put up any horses in the livery stable in the days before Hank's killin', either," Dailey said. "I keep my horse there, and so did Hank, so we would've noticed any strange mounts. Also, Billy Rice, who runs the stable, would've told us if anyone new rode in and boarded their horse. He always let me or Hank know. No out-of-towners bought any supplies from the general store, either. Luke, I know it's frustrating, but except for that hank of hair, the sons of bitches who killed Hank didn't leave a damn clue behind. I'm sorry."

"It's not your fault, so there's no need to apologize," Luke told him. "Mebbe when I go through the house tomorrow I'll come up with somethin'. If not, there's a good possibility Sarah Jane will remember what those men looked like, and give us a good description of 'em. Meantime,

I reckon I'll just have a few more drinks before I turn in."

He drained his glass, slammed it down, refilled it, and drained it yet again.

As the evening progressed, two cowpunchers standing at the opposite end of the bar kept drinking heavily, becoming louder and more obnoxious as they grew drunker. Finally, one of them looked directly at Marshal Dailey.

"Y'know, Marshal," he said, slurring his words. "Me'n Jack are probably the only two people in this town who ain't sorry to see Hank Brundage dead and in the ground. T'warn't right of him, makin' us give those horses back to Lem Tucker. We found those horses, roamin' free on the range. They weren't branded or nothin'."

"You might want to watch your mouth, Staley Harcourt," Dailey warned him. "You and your pardner Jordan there are damn lucky Hank didn't throw both of your sorry butts in jail for horse thievin'. What the hell were you two thinkin'? Everybody in these parts knows those horses are Lem's, and that he doesn't brand 'em."

"Staley, just keep shut, will ya?" his partner pleaded.

"I'll say whatever I damn well please," Harcourt said. "I'm not grievin' our late marshal at all. What I am is jealous of what the *hombres* that finished him off had from his wife. That Sarah Jane is sure easy on the eyes. I'd imagine those boys got some real enjoyment outta the fun they had with her that night. Hell, mebbe when she's up and around again, she'll let me have a good time with her, now that her damn husband's out of the way."

"George . . . ?" Luke said.

"Go ahead, Luke. I damn sure ain't gonna atop you."

"*Gracias.*"

Luke slowly and deliberately placed his glass on the bar, then stalked up to the drunken cowboy, grabbed him by the shoulder, and spun him around.

"You mind repeatin' that, *hombre*?"

"I don't see where what I said is any of your business, Mister."

"Because that's my sister you're talkin' about, runnin' your damn filthy mouth off, you son of a bitch," Luke snapped. He launched a vicious right hook from his hip. The punch caught Harcourt on the point of his chin, lifting him off the floor to land on his back on the bar, out cold.

"You lookin' to get what your pardner got?" Luke asked the other drunk.

"No. No sir, Mister. I didn't say nothin' about your sister, I swear I didn't."

"No, but you didn't shut him up when he was bad-mouthin' my brother-in-law. Didn't happen to disagree with him when he claimed that you were glad Hank was dead, neither."

Luke hit the second man with a powerful left to his jaw, spinning him around and draping him belly down over the bar alongside his unconscious partner. He tried to rise, then fell back, and slid to the sawdust covered floor. His eyes glazed over, then he let out a long sigh as he also lost consciousness.

"I guess that'll teach you two some manners," Luke said, as he rubbed his bruised knuckles.

Dailey had pulled his six-gun, and Martin slid his sawed-off, double-barreled shotgun from under the bar, just in case any friends of the two men thought about starting more trouble. The room had gone silent during the brief altercation; now, conversation started again as most of the patrons went back to their drinking, gambling, or visiting with the percentage girls. The marshal slid his gun back into its holster, the bartender his Greener back into its hiding place.

"Harley, you'd better have one of your boys go fetch Doc Clayton," Dailey said. "Harcourt's jaw appears to be busted. Looks like him and Jordan'll be havin' a nice, long sleep, too."

"Okay, George. Davey . . ."

Martin signaled to one of his swampers, who nodded acknowledgement, then hurried out the door.

"You all right, Luke?" Dailey asked.

"I will be, just got some sore knuckles, that's all. You gonna arrest me, George? I'll go peaceably if you are. Sorry I lost my temper."

"Hell no, I sure ain't," Dailey answered. "Staley Harcourt's been askin' for that for a long time. He's always runnin' off his damn mouth for no good reason. I'm surprised it took this long for someone to almost knock his damn head off. Most of us'll be happy he won't be able to talk for a spell. There's no need for you to apologize, neither. If it had been my sister those two jugheads had been talkin' about, I'd've done a helluva lot worse than taken my fist to 'em. I'd have gut shot both of 'em, right where they stood."

"I appreciate that, George. Harley, I'm sorry about the ruckus. I'll pay for any damages."

"Hell, Luke, the only thing that got busted, besides Harcourt's jaw, was an empty bottle. It was worth that, and more, seein' Harcourt and his pardner get their comeuppances. Your drinks are on the house for the rest of the night."

"I'm obliged, Harley, but if it's all the same to you, I think I'm gonna call it a night. It's been a long couple of days, and I'm plumb tuckered out. Time for some shut-eye. George, you want my statement before I leave?"

"Nope. I was here for the whole thing. I'll just write somethin' up for you to sign in the morning. Go get some sleep."

"Appreciate that. I'll see you first thing tomorrow."

"I'll be ready for you. *Buenas noches*, Luke."

"You too. Night, Harley."

"Good night, Luke. Tell your sister I was askin' for her."

"I'll do that. Thanks."

Luke went straight back to his room in the Sonora House, undressed, and slid under the sheets. He lay staring up at the ceiling for quite some time.

I sure hope Sarah Jane can give me somethin' to go on that'll help me find the sons of bitches I'm after, he thought. *Because right now, I don't have one bit of evidence that I can work with.*

With that unhappy thought, he drifted off to sleep.

Chapter 8

After a breakfast of ham, eggs, and fried potatoes at the hotel's dining room the next morning, Marshal Dailey took Luke over to Hank and Sarah Jane's house.

"This is it," Dailey said, pointing to a small whitewashed structure just off the main street. "No one's been in here since that day, so the house is pretty much still the same inside as when I found Hank's body, and your sister beaten half to death. You ready to see the place? I have to warn you before we go in, it's not a pretty sight."

"I damn sure am," Luke answered.

"All right."

Luke and Dailey walked up to the house. The marshal removed a key from his vest pocket, unlocked the door, and went inside, with Luke just behind him. Dailey closed the door to keep any curious passersby from following them, or peering into the front room.

"It's plain those men were waitin' inside the house for Hank to come home," Dailey said. "They mustn't have left any sign they were about, or Hank would've picked up on it. I figure they surprised him as soon as he walked through the door."

"Uh-huh. Where'd you find Hank and my sister?"

"In the kitchen. This way."

Dailey led Luke through the living room and into the kitchen.

"As I said, Luke, you can see I haven't touched a thing in here, except move a couple piece of furniture to get your sister, and Hank's body, outta the house. I scoured the entire place for evidence, but except for that hunk of hair Sarah Jane was hangin' onto, I didn't find one damn clue. I can tell you she must've put up one helluva a fight before she was beaten senseless."

"I can see she must've," Luke answered. "That'd be Sarah Jane, all right. When we were kids, she could fight better'n half the boys."

Dried blood was spattered throughout the entire room, in some spots pooled. The table was overturned, two of the chairs broken. Pieces of shattered crockery were strewn across the floor. Coffee from the overturned pot left a dark stain on the floor in front of the stove. A shelf hung crookedly from one screw.

"This is where I found Hank," Dailey said, pointing to a long streak of blood down one wall, and a large puddle of dried blood beneath that. "Hard to say whether he died from his busted skull, or the knife wound in his gut."

"From the size of that blood stain on the floor, I'd say he bled out from the belly wound," Luke said. "The one goin' down the wall starts more at the level of a man's head, rather'n his gut. The splatter pattern where it begins looks more like it came from Hank bein' hit with a gun, rather'n blood gushin' from a stab wound. The streak down the wall ain't consistent with a knife wound, either. It's too thin. There's not enough blood for it to have come from a knife. Plus, the puddle on the floor is a couple of feet away from the base of the wall. That indicates two separate wounds, inflicted in slightly different spots. I'd bet my hat Hank was pistol whipped first, then the knife was shoved in his gut. Also, the blood on the floor is dried, on its edge nearest the wall, approximately as if it was stopped by runnin' up against a man lyin' curled up on his side. Hank most likely died slow, and in a whole lot of pain before he passed out. I just hoped he lost consciousness before he knew what happened to Sarah Jane."

"You can tell all that just by lookin' at the bloodstains?" Dailey asked. "Hard to believe. How'd you learn all that?"

Luke shrugged.

"It comes from experience, and learnin' all the time, especially from lawmen older'n smarter than you. Enforcing the law isn't all about fist-fights and tradin' bullets with the bad guys. Most of the time it comes down to usin' your brains more than your brawn, and takin' a careful look-see at everythin' in front of you. You stick with bein' a lawman long enough, and you'll learn, George. Well, lemme take a look around and see what else I might find."

Luke squatted on his haunches next to one of the broken chairs. He pulled a length of rope from underneath it, along with a frayed, red checked bandanna.

"This is most likely the rope those *hombres* used to tie up my sister, and the rag they used to gag her," he said. "They weren't takin' any chances on someone hearin' her scream."

"I figured as much, but never thought findin' those would make a difference," Dailey said. He shook his head. "Boy howdy, any sorry son of a bitch who'd do to a woman what these *hombres* did to Sarah Jane should be stripped buck naked, strung up by his balls first, then dropped down, have his balls cut off while the whole town's watchin', *then* be hung."

"I can't disagree with you there," Luke said. "As far as this rope and cloth, they probably won't help, but you can never tell. Let's see if there's anything more we can come up with."

Luke examined the floor more closely, then looked over the stove. He pulled off a scrap of green and blue striped fabric, which had been caught on one of its corners and torn from a garment.

"This appears to be from a shirt. Does it happen

to match the one Hank was wearin' when you found him?"

"Uh-uh." Dailey shook his head. "He had on a plain brown one. Your sister was wearin' a white blouse. If that *is* a scrap from a shirt, it must've come from one of Hank's killers."

"Most likely it was torn off when Sarah Jane fought back against the *hombre*," Luke answered. He pocketed the cloth, along with the bandanna and length of rope.

"Let's see if there's anythin' else."

It only took a few minutes for Luke to finish going through the kitchen, then the bedroom, the only other room in the house.

"There's nothin' more to find here, George," he said. "You mind showin' me where the horses were hidden?"

"Of course not. It ain't far."

Dailey led Luke around the back of the house.

"You figure those boot prints were left behind by the *hombres* we're lookin' for?" Luke asked, indicating several sets of faded, but still visible, footprints.

"They sure are," Dailey answered. "We haven't had any rain, so they haven't been washed away yet, just scuffed up some by the wind."

"Rain doesn't wash out tracks as easy as most people think it does," Luke answered, as he squatted to study the prints more closely. "I've seen hoof prints after a real gully washer still almost as plain as if it hadn't rained a drop."

He turned to examine one set of tracks more closely.

"Hmpf. One of those men walks with a limp. Already had it before he got here, too. That means Hank or Sarah Jane didn't plug or kick him in the leg."

"You can tell that just by looking at his footprints?"

"Sure. See how the prints his left foot made are just a bit deeper than those made by his right? They show he drags that foot a bit, too. That means one of two things. Either he was limpin', or carryin' somethin' heavy in his left hand. Since the tracks are the same comin' and goin', it's mighty unlikely he was carryin' somethin'."

"You've got sharp eyes."

"I learned a thing or two from the Comanches," Luke answered, without further explanation. "How much farther to where they left the horses?"

"A few hundred feet."

Dailey took Luke to a shallow dry wash. He pointed to a cluster of mesquite, a short distance up the draw.

"This here draw runs for quite a few miles outta town, so it'd be no problem for anyone wantin' to sneak into town to use it for cover, especially if they rode in at night," he explained. "Yonder in that mesquite *bosque* is where they hid the horses."

"Let's take a look."

Once they reached the mesquites, they ducked under the lower branches, into the welcome shade. In the middle of the grove was a patch of ground which had been pounded down by the hooves of waiting horses, which had been stamping with impatience, or at pestering flies. The hungry animals had stripped all the branches within reach of their leaves and pods.

"Those horses were here quite a while," Luke noted.

"Yeah, they damn sure were," Dailey agreed.

Luke plucked a clump of horse hair from a branch.

"This came off a flaxen maned sorrel or chestnut," he said. "Plenty of those in Texas, but nowhere near as common as a bay, or a plain chestnut horse. Let's see what else I might come up with."

He looked at another mesquite, then walked over to it.

"Here. You can see where a good amount of bark has been rubbed off this one's trunk. One of the horses must've gotten an itch, and decided to scratch it by rubbin' against it. What have we got here?"

Luke scuffed up the dirt, then used the toe of his boot to unearth a shiny object which had been just below the surface, barely visible.

"What have you found, Luke?" Dailey asked.

Luke bent down, picked up the object, and held it up, so the sun glinted off it.

"It's a *concho*. A mighty fancy silver one, lots of engraving. It even has four turquoise stones set in it. The horse must've torn it off his saddle when he rubbed against the tree. His rider must've been in too much of a hurry to notice it was missing. Mighty careless of him. Mighty damn careless. This could be a real break. If I can find a saddle decorated with *conchos* like this, but missin' one, that'll place its owner right here. I'll be able to nail him."

Luke looked more closely at the mesquite's trunk. He pulled some strands of leather from its torn bark.

"Black leather. That narrows it down even more. A black saddle with silver and turquoise *conchos*. There ain't too many men who can afford a fancy rig like that."

"Your average cowboy can't, that's for damn certain," Dailey said.

"Let's see if I can come up with anythin' else useful," Luke said.

After more searching, it was plain the horsemen had left no other evidence behind.

"We've done everything we can do here," Luke said. "Let's go talk to my sister."

Luke was surprised to see Sarah Jane not only up and out of bed, but eating a hearty breakfast of scrambled eggs, biscuits, toast, and strong tea.

"Good mornin', Sis. You seem to be a lot better'n yesterday."

"She is," Doctor Clayton said. "I don't quite understand why; however, I'm not questioning it."

"Oh, you men. You think you're so smart, and understand everything, when so many times you haven't a clue," his wife scolded. "Just having a family member nearby can oftentimes make all the difference. Isn't that right, child?"

"That, and your good cooking, Clarissa," Sarah Jane answered. "These are the best scrambled eggs I've ever eaten. They are so tasty I finally got my appetite back. And yes, Luke, I'm feeling much better, thank you."

"So I guess you don't need me here, long as you've got the doc's wife's meals," Luke said, grinning. "I reckon I'll just mosey on down the trail, then."

"Don't you dare, Luke," Sarah Jane retorted. "I'm sure you have plenty of questions for me. I'm ready to answer them now."

"Not until you finish your breakfast," Clayton said. "You still need to make up for the past few days, when you've barely eaten a bite."

"Doctor's orders?" Sarah Jane asked.

"No. The doctor's *wife's* orders," Clayton answered. "They carry even more weight than mine."

"Ranger, would you also like some breakfast?" Clarissa asked.

"No thank you, ma'am. Me'n Marshal Dailey just had ours, at the hotel's dining room. I'll just step outside and have a smoke, while Sarah Jane finishes hers, that is, if you don't mind, Sis."

"Not at all," Sarah Jane answered. "I'd feel rushed with you standing there, watching my every bite, tryin' to hurry me along."

"I'll join you, Ranger," Clayton said. "It's about time for my morning pipe anyway. I'll enjoy having company while I relax and smoke."

"That's fine with me," Luke said. They headed onto the front porch.

"I have to admit, Ranger," Clayton said, once he had his pipe going, "I was more than surprised to see the improvement in your sister's condition this morning. It's as if she turned the corner overnight, and is well on her way to recovery. The only explanation I have is your presence. Quite often, having a family member, or loved one, nearby will give a sick or injured person the will to live. Were you and Sarah Jane very close as you were growing up?"

"Yeah, I guess you could say that. Our folks didn't have any other kids, so it was just the two of us, and we're only a year apart in age. Mostly, we'd get into trouble a lot, or I guess mischief would be more accurate a word. Both of us liked exploring, so we'd wander off more than our ma and pa would've liked. It wasn't until I got married that we spent much time apart. And of course after I joined the Rangers we saw even less of each other."

"I know your parents have both died, so now, with Hank gone, you're the only family she's got."

"Me and my wife and kids. We've got two boys and two girls," Luke said. "I'm hopin' mebbe, once she's feelin' better and things have settled some, Sarah Jane will go stay with Addie and my children for a spell, at least until I get back from chasin' down the men who did this."

"That's an excellent idea. Your sister has friends here in Sonora, of course, but in a situation such as this, it's usually better for a person to be with family. I'll suggest it as soon as I feel it's the right time."

"I appreciate that, Doc."

Luke took a last drag on his quirly, then tossed the butt into the dirt.

"You reckon Sarah Jane's done with her breakfast?"

"If not, she must be just about finished," Clayton answered. "Let's go find out."

Sarah Jane had just finished her meal when they walked back into her room.

"I was just coming to get you," Clarissa said. "William, Sarah Jane has requested that you allow her to remain out of bed for a short amount of time, while she visits with her brother."

"That will be fine, as long as you don't overtax yourself, Sarah Jane," Clayton answered. "I'll pop back in and check on you in about thirty minutes. If you're not feeling weak by then, I'll allow you a bit more time."

"Thank you, Doctor," Sarah Jane said.

"Yeah, thanks, Doc," Luke added. "We're obliged."

"Sarah Jane, if you start to feel weak or dizzy, have Luke come get me immediately."

"I will, Doctor."

"Fine, then I'll leave you with your brother."

Luke sat down, but didn't speak until the doctor and his wife had left.

"You really do look much better, Sis," he said.

"I am feeling better, at least for now," she answered.

"I hate to do this to you so quick, but the doc didn't give us a heckuva lot of time to talk. I've got to ask you what you recall about the day Hank was killed, and you were, um, violated."

"I was raped," Sarah Jane said, softly but sharply. "You can say the word, Luke. A word can't possibly hurt me more than what those men did, so don't you dare try and sugarcoat what happened."

"All right. I'm sorry. I was just tryin' to avoid making you feel even worse. Are you ready to answer some questions for me, because right now,

I don't have a dang thing to go on, except the hair Marshal Dailey found in your hand, and a piece of blue and green striped cloth that's probably from one of the attackers' shirts. I'm countin' on you to come up with enough information I can identify the men involved, or at least get a good idea what they looked like. Unless you can give me some help, I don't have any idea where to start lookin' for those *hombres*, let alone who they were. How much of that day do you think you can remember?"

"Luke, I remember every minute of that day as if it just happened. I can describe the men, almost every detail of what they did to me and Hank, at least before I passed out, and even some of their names."

"That's what I need, all right," Luke answered. "I'm not going to ask you any questions, at least right off. Just tell me in your own words what happened that day. Take your time, and if you need to pause, to gather your emotions or thoughts, or just rest, you stop, then resume your story when you're ready. And if it becomes too much for you, and you need to quit for the day, just say so. All right?"

"That's fine. I need to talk about that day anyway. I've been keeping everything inside me for so long I feel as if I'm about to burst. I just couldn't bring myself to talk to anyone else but you, Luke."

Sarah Jane sighed, and stifled a sob.

"I . . . I still don't know if I can do this," she said.

Luke patted her shoulder. She cringed.

"Of course you can, Sis," he encouraged her. "You're one of the strongest persons, male or female, I've ever known. I'm not sayin' that just because you're my sister, either. So take as much time as you need, but tell me everything you can, so I can track down the sons of bit . . . um, the no-good skunks who are responsible for Hank's death. As you just said, you'll probably feel better once you get things off your chest."

"All right. I think I'm ready now," Sarah Jane answered. "Those men must have been watching the house, waiting for me to go out, so they could sneak in while I was gone. There was no sign of them when I left for a visit with old Gertrude Carmody. She's been all alone since her husband Joe passed away last year, with all her children gone off East somewhere. Her daughter wanted her to move back to Virginia and live with her and her family, but Gertrude said no, her home is right here in Sonora, that her husband is buried here, and when her time came she was going to be laid to rest right alongside him. So, since I know she's lonely, I baked a peach cobbler and took it over to her. We had a delightful chat over coffee and cobbler. Oh, I'm sorry, prattling on and on like this, when I should be getting right to the point. You don't need to hear all the silly little things I did earlier."

"No, you're doing just fine," Luke assured her. "You need to tell the story any way you're most comfortable. Besides, you never know when talking about what you did earlier might jolt your memory, and you'll recollect some little detail that turns out to be the clue I need. So just go ahead."

Sarah Jane took a deep breath, then continued.

"Nothing appeared out of place when I arrived back home. However, when I walked inside, a man, who was hiding against the wall behind the door, grabbed me from behind, and held his hand over my mouth. He warned me not to scream, as if I could with my mouth clamped shut and him squeezing me so tightly I couldn't breathe. When he asked if I understood, all I could do was nod. Then he pushed me into the kitchen. Four other men were waiting in there. They tied me to a chair, and told me I wouldn't get hurt as long as I listened to them, and didn't cause any trouble. I told them I wouldn't, but the leader ordered one of the others to gag me anyway."

"You didn't try'n fight them, did you?"

Sarah Jane shook her head.

"No, I wanted to, in the worst way, but they had me tied too tightly to even think about attempting to break loose. At least one of them always had a gun on me, too, so I'd have been shot dead before I could escape anyway."

"You did the right thing, Sis. I'm also certain the only reason you were gagged was to keep you from cryin' out a warnin' to Hank."

"I wish I'd tried after all. What those men did was far worse than just killin' me. They killed my husband, and while he was dying they took turns raping me. Hank lived long enough to see most of what they did. He must have hated me for letting those evil men have their way with me. Oh, I feel so ashamed. So guilty about not being able to save Hank. So, so . . . *dirty!*"

She began crying again. When Luke placed a hand on her arm to comfort her, she shrank back.

"Don't. Please, don't touch me," Sarah Jane pleaded.

"Okay, I'm sorry," Luke said. "You shouldn't feel ashamed. Or guilty. What happened was not your fault. Those men were there for one reason, to murder Hank in cold blood. You, unfortunately, were the easiest way for them to get to Hank, except mebbe for shooting him in the back from ambush. I'm pretty sure everything they did was part of their plan. They *wanted* Hank to die slow, and make him suffer as much as possible, it seems to me. What better way to do that than by attacking you while he was dyin'? I'm sorry to say, there's nothin' you could have done. Whoever the men are who did this, they planned the whole thing very well. They're lower than rabid coyotes, and need to be gunned down the same as you would one of them."

"I keep trying to tell myself that, but it isn't easy."

"I know. Listen, I really hate to put you through this, and if you're not ready to continue right now, say so, but I need you to tell me, as best you recollect, everything which happened that day. I don't need you to go into all the details of say, the assaults on you, or anything that's too hard for you to relate, but I've gotta have as much information as you can give me. You're the key to finding those men. Can you do it?"

"I'll do anything I have to, to make certain they face a noose," Sarah Jane answered.

"Good. That's the sister I know," Luke said. "Whenever you're ready. Skip ahead to when Hank got home."

"All right. As I've said, I had no way to warn Hank those men were in the house, waiting for him. One of them was hidden behind the door. As soon as Hank walked in, he stuck his gun in Hank's back, and disarmed him. When Hank was brought into the kitchen and saw me, he tried to reach me. One of the other men, the leader, kicked him in his privates, then, when Hank fell, kicked him again, in the belly. Hank was helpless after that. Oh, it was awful!"

"Take your time, Sis," Luke urged. "Rest a spell if you need to."

"No." Sarah Jane shook her head. "I want to, I need to, get this over with."

"Okay. Go ahead."

"Anyway, Hank was kicked and punched some more, then dragged to his feet. The leader told him to do everything they wanted or they'd slice me up with their knives. Then he told me, if I cooperated, they might let Hank live. When I said I didn't believe him, he said he didn't care. To prove it, he had one of the other men stick a gun in Hank's mouth, and threatened to put a bullet through Hank's head unless I did exactly what they told me. Hank told me not to listen, that they were going to kill him no matter what, but I had to try and save him, even though I knew he was right. But, when that awful man started to unbutton my blouse, I slapped his face. I couldn't help myself. Maybe if I'd just . . ."

Her voice trailed off.

"Sarah Jane, listen to me," Luke said. "Do you think Hank would have wanted you to give in to those men without a fight? No, he sure wouldn't have. You did exactly what he would want you to do, fight as hard as you could."

"I know. He told me that, too."

"See, there you are. So what happened next?"

"After I slapped that man, he ripped open my blouse. When he did, I clawed at his face. I think

I poked one of his eyes out, at least he screamed at me that I had. I know I sliced open both his cheeks pretty well. Then he punched me in the stomach. I couldn't breathe, so everything after that is a blur. I saw Hank try to reach me, but the man guarding him hit him over the head with his gun, then stabbed him. Then I remember being shoved to the floor, and a man on top of me, then another, and another. After that, I must have passed out, because I don't remember anything until I woke up here, at the doctor's."

"You don't need to say anything else, Sis," Luke said. "I can fill in the rest by myself. Do you need to stop for a few minutes? Should I call the doc, or perhaps get you some water or tea?"

"No. Please, let's get this finished," Sarah Jane answered. "You must have some questions?"

"I do. First, you mentioned you had some names. What are they?"

"Hank recognized the leader of the gang. He called him 'Williams.' That must be his last name, because the man who killed Hank called him Hutch. That man's first name was Mace. He and Hutch are brothers."

"How about the others?"

"I only heard their first names. There was a Jody, and a Brian. I'm not certain if Brian was his first or last name, or spelled with a y, not an i. The last one was called Slate. Again, I don't know if that was his first or last name."

"It doesn't matter. You've given me a good place to start. Did any of 'em happen to mention why they wanted Hank dead?"

"No. No, they didn't. He didn't get the chance to say, either, before they killed him."

"And you didn't recognize any of the men, or their names?"

"No. I was hoping you would."

"So was I, but I don't. Whoever they are, Hank must have had dealin's with 'em before I knew him. He never liked to talk about the *hombres* he'd tangled with in the past. This is one time I wish he had. Nothin' to be done for it. Those names, especially the two brothers, are good, solid leads. Soon as we're done, I'll go over to the Western Union office, and send wires to both Ranger Headquarters and the state penitentiary in Huntsville. Odds are one of those places will have records of Hank's killers. All his cases will be on file in Austin, and Huntsville will have records of any men with those names who were prisoners there. Can I ask you just a couple more questions?"

"I'm feeling a bit tired, but please, yes. I want to get this behind me and move on."

"I understand. When the marshal found you, you were holding a hank of reddish blond hair. You must have pulled it out of one of those *hombres*. Do you remember that? And what he looked like?"

"I think so. He was the third man, and hurt me more than the two brothers, who took their turns at me first. He was so rough, I had to try and get him off me, so I grabbed his hair, since it was quite long. He also had a ginger colored mustache. I remember feeling it against my face. He had the most evil eyes, too. Brown, but kind of a yellowish brown. They looked like they belonged to a snake."

"They did. A two legged snake. One that walks upright instead of crawls on its belly," Luke said. "Do you know which man that was?"

"It was the one Hutch Williams called 'Slate.' "

"Good. I'll make certain he gets special treatment before I bring him in. Can you describe any of the others?"

"I most certainly can. I'll never forget their faces. The two brothers looked almost exactly alike. They had dark brown hair and eyes. Both were slim, and not tall, but not short, either, just about average height. The one called Mace was a bit shorter. He was the younger of the two, it appeared, probably by two or three years."

"And it seems like Hutch will have some nasty scars from your fingernails," Luke added. "Plus, if you really did poke one of his eyes out, he'll be wearin' an eye patch. That'll make him easy to pick out. How about the last two?"

"Jody was blond, with pale blue eyes. He was very tall, probably over six feet, and really skinny. Brian was also tall, but fat. For some reason, he took off his shirt before he had his way with me. He had a big belly, which felt so disgusting when he got on top of me. He was a real pig, who sweated a lot. He had sandy hair and gray eyes. Oh, and he was the one wearing a striped shirt. I remember that now."

"Which probably means that shirt got torn off when he caught it on the stove. It has to be his shirt the scrap of cloth came from. He didn't take it off, at least not on purpose. Sis, that's enough for now. It seems like more things are starting to come back to you. When they do, tell the doc, or his wife, and have one of 'em write them down for me."

"You're not leaving me, Luke?"

"Only for a little while. I've got to get those telegrams off. With any luck, I'll get my answers back today, or first thing tomorrow morning. I'll come back to see you later this afternoon, after you've gotten some more rest."

"Luke?"

"Yeah, Sis?"

"You will find those men, won't you?"

"You can bet your hat on it. Once I find out who they are for certain, I'll have every lawman in Texas lookin' for 'em. But I intend to get to 'em first."

He bent down and gave Sarah Jane a kiss on the cheek.

"I've gotta go. I'll send the doc in on my way out."

"Luke?"

"Somethin' else?"

"Just . . . thank you."

"All part of my job as a Ranger. But this one's personal. See you later."

Chapter 9

The answers to Luke's messages didn't arrive until late the next afternoon. While he waited, he visited with Sarah Jane for much of the morning, then he once again went through the house where Hank had been murdered. After that, he spent the rest of the day talking with the residents of Sonora, hoping that someone, anyone, might have seen something that would help him track down the men who had raped his sister and killed her husband. The killers had covered their trail well. Not one person recalled seeing any strangers ride into or out of town, nor anyone suspicious near the Brundage house. Frustrated, Luke returned to the Western Union office. He waited impatiently, pestering the operator, until the telegraph key finally began chattering.

"Is that from . . . ?" he began. The telegrapher, hunched over his receiver, frantically transcribing the Morse code signal into words, waved Luke off. After what seemed an eternity to Luke, the long message concluded, and the key finally fell silent. The telegrapher transmitted a reply acknowledging receipt, then leaned back in his chair. He pushed his green eyeshade back from his forehead.

"Here you go, Ranger," he said, handing Luke

several yellow flimsies. "I hope it's what you wanted."

Luke quickly scanned the copy.

"It sure is. Thanks."

The telegraph key began chattering again.

"Hold on just a minute," the telegrapher told Luke. "This one might be for you, also." He listened to the first few clicks of the key, then grabbed his pencil.

"Yep, it's from Huntsville," he said, as he began scribbling down the message. Three minutes later, he handed another sheet of paper to Luke.

"That's both your answers. Good luck, Ranger. I hope you find the bastards."

"I will. You can count on it."

Luke tossed the man a dime tip, then hurried out the door, and up the road to Doctor Clayton's. He knocked on the door, shifting impatiently from one foot to the other while he waited for someone to answer. The door opened.

"Ranger Caldwell, there you are," Clarissa Clayton said. "My husband and I were hoping you'd return soon. Your sister has been worried that something might have happened to you. Please, come right in. You know where Sarah Jane's room is at. I'll fetch my husband."

"Thank you, ma'am," Luke answered. He removed his hat as he stepped through the door, then hurried down the hall to Sarah Jane's room.

"I'm back, Sis, just like a bad penny," he said.

"Luke!" Sarah Jane sat bolt upright in her bed. "I've been so afraid for you."

"So Mrs. Clayton told me," he said, smiling. "You needn't have worried."

"You can't blame me, though. I've already lost Hank. I couldn't stand it if one of those men had stumbled across you and killed you, too."

"Those men are long gone," Luke answered. "They weren't about to hang around town after they finished the job they came to do."

"Does that mean you have news?"

"I sure do, Sis. Hutchinson and Mason Williams are brothers, as you said. Their father is Zachary Williams. He owns the largest ranch in Val Verde County. Hank arrested Hutch for killin' a cowboy in a gunfight over a saloon gal down in Comstock. Hutch claimed the other man had drawn first, but Hank saw the fight firsthand. His testimony stated Hutch challenged the cowboy to a fight, then pulled his gun. The cowboy was just a kid, seventeen years old. His hand had barely started for his gun before Hutch shot him three times. When Hank went to arrest Hutch, his brother tried to stop him. Hank plugged him in the leg. That jibes with the footprints I saw, back of your house. One of the men walked with a limp. That had to be Mason. Hank arrested him too."

"So why weren't they hung, or at least given life in prison?" Sarah Jane asked.

"Mason wouldn't have faced more'n about five or ten years, for interfering with a peace officer in the performance of his duties, and obstruction of justice. He claimed the charges were trumped up, that he was only tryin' to calm his brother down. As far as Hutch, you're absolutely right. He should have hung. However, everybody else in the saloon claimed Hank didn't see the fight start, and the kid had drawn first. The Williams brothers were found not guilty. Hutch did make threats against Hank's life, but hell—I'm sorry for cussin', Sis—I mean, heck, lawmen hear threats like that all the time. They usually don't mean nothin'."

"Still, Hank should have arrested Hutch for making those threats."

"Mebbe, but it'd take more than just some angry words to convince a prosecutor to even bring charges. Worse, I've already said the Williams boys' father owns the biggest spread in Val Verde County. He's got plenty of money, and influence. He built a town and named it after himself. Even convinced the Galveston, Harrisburg, and San Antonio Railroad to build a spur from Comstock out to his ranch. He hired the best lawyers he could find for his two boys. I'm also positive the witnesses were either bought off, or threatened. Not many people would stand up to a man like Zach Williams. They'd be certain to lose their jobs, homes, businesses, or worse.

So yeah, they're both guilty as sin, and the trial was a joke. That doesn't matter now. What does matter is findin' those two and bringin' 'em in for Hank's murder, and the attack on you. This time, the charges will stick. I promise you that, Sis."

"You can't guarantee that. Not if their father has as much power as you say, Luke."

"I do, Sarah Jane. The Williams brothers will pay the price for what they've done, one way or the other."

"I hope you're right, little brother. I want to see them dead. What about the other three men?"

"I was just comin' to them. The man you called Slate is a gunslinger out of Kansas, name of Slate Martin. He's a killer for hire, so odds are the Williamses heard of his reputation, and hired him to help kill Hank. As far as the last two, neither Austin nor Huntsville has anythin' on 'em. They're most likely a couple of Williams's cowboys who were ordered to come along."

"Neither of them actually took part in Hank's murder," Sarah Jane said. "It was the other three who did that."

"It doesn't matter. They backed the Williamses' play, so they're both guilty as hell, um, heck," Luke answered. "Besides, you said all five of them took a turn at you."

"That's right, they did. I want it made certain they can never do to another woman what they did to me."

"There you have it. I doubt any jury would let them off without hangin', but you can be certain at the very least even Jody and Brian will spend the rest of their lives behind bars."

"Luke?" Sarah Jane's voice was just above a whisper.

"Yeah, Sis?"

"You said you were goin' to arrest those men, and bring them back for trial?"

"That's right, unless they put up a fight. In which case, I'll put bullets through every last one of 'em, and drop 'em right where they stand."

"Luke, I want those men dead. I want them to die slowly and painfully, just like Hank died. I want them to die a thousand deaths, as I've done every day since they turned my life upside down."

"You think I don't? I'd like nothin' better'n to sink a couple .45 slugs in each of their guts, and watch them die in front of me. Nothin' would give me more pleasure. But I'm a lawman, a Texas Ranger sworn to uphold the law. If I kill those men in cold blood, I'll be no better than they are."

"Couldn't you just shoot them, and say they were attempting to escape?"

"I could, but I won't. My conscience wouldn't let me."

"Even after what they did to Hank? To me, your only sister?"

"Even after that. Sis, look at it this way. Havin' to face a judge and jury, knowin' the entire state of Texas will hear the whole sordid story of what they did, then sweatin' before the noose is tied around their necks and the trap door drops, will be even worse punishment than bein' gut-shot."

"I don't want to wait and see if somehow they get off, like you said they did when they killed that young cowboy. I couldn't live, knowing they were walking around free, while my husband is dead and buried."

Sarah Jane burst into tears.

"I know," Luke said. "I can't say I can even imagine what you're goin' through, but I understand your feelings. If it were up to me, I'd gun them down. But it's not."

Sarah Jane stopped crying, then fixed Luke with a steady gaze.

"I want to come with you."

"What?"

"You heard me, Luke. I want to come with you. I want to help you find those men. I want to see them face to face. I want them to know that they haven't taken everything from me, that I've survived, and will see them dead!"

"You can't, Sis. It's impossible. Even if I agreed, you're in no shape for a long, hard ride. I'll be traveling as fast as I can. That means all day in the saddle, sleepin' on the hard ground at night, nothin' to eat but bacon and beans, then start the whole thing over again the next mornin', until I come up with those *hombres*. You'd only slow me down."

"I would not," Sarah Jane insisted. "I'm doing much better. Yes, I'm sore from the beating I took, but no more sore than if I'd fallen off a horse. I've got Hank's horse, and his gun, unless those men took them. And I've got enough anger, deep in my soul, to give me the strength I need."

"No, they didn't take Hank's horse and six-gun."

"So I have a good horse, and a gun. Hank taught me how to shoot, and I already know how to ride almost as well as you do, so there's no reason I can't come along. I'll have you know I'm pretty handy with a rifle, too."

"Yes, there is. You're a woman. This is man's work. I'll probably have to go into saloons, maybe even bawdy houses, lookin' for those *hombres*. You can't go into places like that."

"The hell I can't."

"Sarah Jane! If Ma or Pa ever heard you cussin' . . ."

"Stop trying to coddle me, little brother, I've heard men curse, and I've seen plenty of men drunk, including you and Pa. Hank too. I also know what goes on in those brothels. I'm not some innocent little china doll, to be put under a glass dome on a shelf over the fireplace."

"You still can't come. I forbid it."

Sarah Jane's anger flared.

"Perhaps I didn't make myself clear. I'm going with you, Luke, and that's that. No argument. Don't try to tell me it's not allowed by the Rangers, either. I know, as well as you do, any Ranger can ask a citizen to volunteer, at any time. And you don't own me. You have no right to forbid me to go anywhere, or do anything I want. Don't even suggest you're doing this to protect me. I don't need protection from any man. I'm more than capable of taking care of myself, thank you very much."

"A male citizen."

"That's not what the rulebook says. Hank showed it to me. It says 'any citizen.' If you don't take me with you, I'll follow you, or I'll strike out after those men on my own. You can't stop me."

"Sarah Jane, think. If you did that, the best that could happen is you'd scare them off, and they'd never be caught. The worst is they could rape you again, then make certain you were dead this time."

"With you, little brother, or alone?"

"There's no changing your mind?"

"Not a snowball's chance in Hell."

Luke rubbed his chin before answering.

"Mebbe it could work. If you wore loose clothes, and kept your voice low, I might could pass you off as my kid brother. Disguising you as a man would never work. You can't grow a beard, your skin's too smooth, and your voice is too high. Sooner or later, someone'd catch on."

"I'm not goin' as a man, Luke. I'm goin' as a woman, a woman who's mad as hell. A woman who will make certain those men pay for what they did to me. That's the only way I'll be able to put at least part of this ordeal behind me, and start my life again. I'll wear a man's shirt and pants, since they'll be more practical than a split ridin' skirt and a blouse for the trip, but I'm goin' as a woman."

"I could have you tossed in jail," Luke said, now grinning. "A witness to a crime who needs protective custody."

"But you won't."

"No, I won't. I can see this is something you have to do. I guess I'd feel the same way, if I were in your boots. Tell you what. As long as Doc Clayton says it's okay, you can side me. We can wait another day or two before leavin' if he thinks you need a bit more time to recover."

"Won't that give those men more time to get away?"

Luke shook his head.

"Nope. A couple more days won't make a difference. I'm certain they didn't go anywhere, except back to their father's ranch. They figure they're safe there, and up until now, they've been right. That's gonna change. They're about to find out exactly how mistaken they are."

"Luke, thank you. Honestly, I didn't think I could convince you."

"Wait until this is all over before you thank me, Sis. By the time this is finished, we may both be sorry. As far as convincin' me, I could see you had your mind set, and there was no way I could change it. I can't really blame you. Sometimes, livin' can be worse'n dyin'. Listen, I think it'd be better if you talk to the doc alone. I'll send him in. I'm gonna pick up some more supplies for the trail. Is there anything I can get you?"

"Yes. I need lipstick, lots of rouge, and a low cut gown, for when we go into those brothels. Some perfume, too. I may need to act like a scarlet woman to help find those men. I don't think you could pull that off."

"Sorry, Sis, that's where I draw the line. You want Ma and Pa to come back and haunt me for the rest of my life?"

"I was only kidding, Luke. Just make certain you have enough ammunition and food for both of us. I can use a new pair of denim pants. Yes, I wear pants, or split riding skirts. Don't look so shocked. We're not back East, where ladies only wear long skirts and ride those ridiculous sidesaddles. Miriam at the store knows my size. Would you ask her to come by here when she has a minute? I'll make up a list of things I need from the house. I'm not ready to go back there quite yet. Oh, and get me some peppermint sticks and lemon drops. I truly love those. And some tea."

"Tea?"

"Yes, tea."

"Our parents always said you were headstrong, Sis. Reckon I always knew it too, just didn't want to admit *how* headstrong. I'll send the doc in, then fetch the supplies. I'll make certain Hank's horse is ready to travel, too. I'll have the blacksmith replace his shoes, all around. No sense in riskin' him throwin' a shoe on the trail. You're sure about this? I can't change your mind?"

"Nope."

"Then get ready to ride, pardner."

Chapter 10

Two days later, after visiting Hank's grave, giving both of them the chance to say a final good-bye, Luke and Sarah Jane were in the saddle, making their farewells to the Claytons and Marshal Dailey.

"Sarah Jane, don't you forget what I said," Doctor Clayton warned her. "If you feel ill, particularly if you become nauseous, light-headed, or start spitting up blood, you immediately find the nearest town with a physician."

"I'll do that, Doctor," Sarah Jane promised. "However, you needn't fret about me. If I survived what those men did to me, I can certainly handle a ride to Val Verde County. I assure you I'll find a way to thank you and Clarissa properly once I return home."

"Just seeing you getting well is thanks enough," Clarissa answered.

"It's what happens when you get to Val Verde County that I'm worried about," Dailey said. "I still think this is a plumb fool idea, Sarah Jane."

"Don't worry about me, Marshal," she answered. "I've got my little brother Luke Caldwell, the big, tough Texas Ranger lieutenant to protect me. I'll be just fine."

"Yes, but what about Luke? Who's going to

protect him from you?" Clarissa asked, with a soft laugh.

"You have to admit, she's got a point, Sis," Luke said.

"Oh, go on with all of you."

"Speaking of goin', we'd better do just that," Luke said. "It's ninety miles, give or take, and a three day ride to Williams City. George, thanks for all your help, and for lookin' after the house for Sarah Jane until we get back. Doc, Mrs. Clayton, I'm especially obliged to you both for pullin' my sister through."

"We had a lot of help from God," Clayton said.

"I won't argue with you there," Luke said.

"Sarah Jane, Luke, I'll pray for your safe return, and that the men responsible are brought to justice," Clarissa said.

"We all will," Clayton added.

"That's all we can ask," Luke said. He touched two fingers to the brim of his hat in farewell. "*Adios*."

"*Vaya con Dios*," Dailey shouted.

"Let's go, Sis."

Luke put Pete into a walk, with RePete, carrying the pack saddle, trailing behind, and Sarah Jane, mounted on Casey, her late husband's stocky, blaze-faced bay quarter horse gelding, alongside her brother. She was dressed in a red woolen shirt, a pair of men's denim pants, and brown boots. A tan wide brimmed hat, held in place by a cord knotted under her chin, covered her hair. She had Hank's gun belt wrapped around her waist, his .45 Colt SAA Army Peacemaker in the holster that rode at her right hip. His Model 1873 Winchester rode in a saddle scabbard under her left leg.

"Soon as we let the horses warm up, I'll pick up the pace," Luke said. "Let me know if it gets too tough for you, and we'll take a rest."

"The only time we'll need to stop is when *you* can't keep up with *me,* little brother."

"Oh, is that right?"

"That's right."

Luke kept his horses, who were eager to run after their days of rest, at a walk until they reached the edge of town. He put them into a slow jogtrot, then, after a quarter mile, an easy lope. He glanced over at his sister, who put Casey into the same gait, matching Luke's horses stride for stride. Luke looked sideward at her, scowled, and shook his head.

"Well, I'll be damned," he muttered, under his breath. He kicked Pete into an even faster, mile-eating lope.

Chapter 11

Ordinarily, Luke would have made the trek from Sonora to Williams City in two days or a little more, switching between his two horses during brief rest stops, stopping for the night well after dark, then being back in the saddle before sunup the next morning. However, with his own injuries still healing, and certain the ride was taxing on his sister, no matter how hard she attempted to hide her exhaustion, he decided to call a halt for the night about an hour before sundown.

"Why are we stopping so soon?" Sarah Jane asked. "There's still plenty of daylight left."

"Three reasons," Luke answered. "First, whether you want to admit it or not, you need to rest. You can't allow yourself to overdo things, since you've been laid up for a spell. I can use a good night's sleep too. Second, more importantly, the horses need rest, especially Casey. I'm sure he didn't go on many long chases once Hank became a town marshal, so he needs time to get back in shape. Third, and most important, there's a waterhole here. Those are few and far between out this way. So we'll camp for the night here, then push a little harder tomorrow. All right?"

"You know the territory far better than I do, Luke. I just hate to think those men might get away because we weren't quick enough catching up with them."

"I'm as anxious to get them as you are, Sis. But pushing too hard, so we end up having to take an extended rest, giving them even more time to put distance between us, is taking a bigger chance than pacing ourselves. I'm not worried about them running any farther than the Williams spread in any event. They no doubt believe that besides Hank, they also killed you, or left you so crippled you wouldn't be able to testify against 'em. They also know their pa will do anythin' he has to do to protect them. And since no one else saw 'em in Sonora, I'm positive they'll have a nice, airtight alibi showing they were right at home the entire time. They're not one bit worried about anyone bein' on their trail. That'll be the mistake that trips 'em up. So let's dismount and get these horses taken care of. After that, I'll make supper, then we'll turn in early."

"Okay, Luke. I have to admit, getting out of this saddle will feel wonderful. Some food will sure taste good, too."

"You might want to wait until you sample my cookin' until you decide on that," Luke said, with a chuckle. When he started to dismount, swinging his right leg over Pete's rump, a sharp pain shot through his gut. He doubled up, and fell hard on his back. He lay there, trying to force air back into his lungs. Pete dropped his head to begin nuzzling Luke's face, then swiped his huge pink tongue over it.

"Luke!" Sarah Jane cried. She jumped off Casey and ran up to her brother. "What happened? Are you all right?"

"I will be . . . if these two cussed jugheads don't drown me," Luke answered. RePete had now joined his brother in attempting to get Luke up, pushing his nose under Luke's side and shoving. "G'wan, get out of here, both of you, unless you want to become dog food."

Unable to control her mirth, Sarah Jane laughed while Luke struggled to shove the two paints aside.

"I'm sorry, Luke, but you just look so funny lyin' there, with those horses washing your face. Are you certain you're all right?"

Luke gave Pete a slap on the neck. The horse finally moved aside, dropping his head to nibble at the grass.

"I am. It was only a stitch in my side, that's all. Just got the wind knocked outta me when I fell. Gimme a hand up, will you?"

"Sure."

Sarah Jane took Luke's extended right hand and helped him stand up. He stood hunched over, and took in several deep breaths.

"There. Got my air back. I'm fine now."

"Don't you scare me like that again, Luke."

"Hey, it wasn't much fun for me, either. Let's

give these horses a drink, then get the gear off 'em and rub 'em down."

The waterhole Luke had chosen was merely a small *cienega*, a seep from the bottom of a low bluff, which formed a small pool, the water trickling from its outlet sinking into the sand and evaporating before going five yards. After the horses drank, Luke and Sarah Jane had to wait for the pool to refill before they could get their own drinks. After pulling the gear off their horses, they curried them thoroughly, then cleaned out their hooves, making certain there were no pebbles lodged between the frog and sole that could bruise a hoof and lame a mount. Once that was done, the horses were picketed where they could crop at the sparse grass surrounding the seep. Luke took a sack of grain from the pack saddle, and poured out a small amount for each animal. Once the horses were cared for, Luke and Sarah Jane could attend to their own needs. Luke gathered some fallen, dry mesquite branches to make a small, almost smokeless fire.

"Luke, can I help you do anything?" Sarah Jane asked.

"No, you just take it easy, Sis," he answered. "I'll have the coffee boilin', the bacon and beans fryin', and the biscuits in the pan in two shakes."

"If you insist."

"I do. I'm used to cookin' on the trail, so it's pretty easy for me."

In a short while, Luke was filling tin plates with bacon, beans, and biscuits, and tin mugs with hot, black coffee.

"Do you want the peppermint stick from the Arbuckle's, Sis?" he asked. "If not, I'm gonna break it in half and save it for Pete and RePete."

"No, thank you. I've got the candy you bought for me. Save that one for your horses."

"*Gracias*. They do enjoy getting a treat."

Luke passed Sarah Jane her plate and mug. They sat cross-legged next to the fire.

"Luke, this isn't bad at all," Sarah Jane said, after a few mouthfuls. "It's hardly gourmet cooking, but it's tasty, and I'd imagine pretty filling."

"I can handle bacon and beans all right. Just don't ask me to try anythin' more complicated, except mebbe a beefsteak and fried taters. I can also do a fair job with any game I might shoot."

"I have to admit, I was so hungry almost anything would taste good."

"Be careful what you wish for," Luke advised. "If things get too tough, we might have to eat rattlesnake, or grubs."

"Then I'll eat rattlesnake or grubs."

"Boy howdy, you've sure changed, Sis. You're not the dainty little thing you were when I left to join the Rangers. Back in those days, you were all satin and lace, and oh so proper. What happened?"

"That woman you remember was what Mother wanted, not me," Sarah Jane explained. "Father too. I just couldn't work up the courage to stand up to them, especially since they expected me to marry a professional man, one who could take over Father's accounting firm. Later, after they passed on, and I married Hank, I was finally able to become the woman *I* wanted to be, not some genteel lady, who does all the proper things that society expects a woman to do, and associates with only the best people."

"But we lived in Junction," Luke objected. "Folks ain't all citified and hoity-toity in a place like Junction."

"Of course they are, Luke. Sometimes they're even worse in a small town. You know most of the women would never even nod at a working girl from the saloons, let alone speak to one. They were even condescending to the ladies who clerked in the stores, or ran their own shops, such as the millinery or dress shops. Heaven forbid if I had even set one foot inside a saloon. The women who formed the Ladies' Civic Improvement Society of Junction are some of the worst, always looking down their noses at everyone. After you defied Mother and Father, and left home to join the Rangers, things got even worse for me. All the plans Father had for you to follow in his footsteps became my burden. Mother made it her mission to find me the right kind of man to marry. I loved Mother and Father, deeply, but Heaven forgive me, after they died and once I was through mourning, I felt more free than I'd ever felt in my life."

"I'm sorry, Sis. I didn't realize you were that unhappy."

"Not so much unhappy, as frustrated. I never said anything to you, because you had enough trouble breaking away. I was afraid if I had pleaded with you not to go, you would have stayed home, and gone to work with Father. I knew you could never be happy with an office job. You have a wild streak that can never be tamed. It will never let you stay in one place for long. Besides, I realized I wouldn't be stuck in Junction forever. The few years Hank and I had together were the happiest of my life."

"Yeah, you're right about that. Even after I married Addie, and even after we had the kids, I still had to be on the move after a few days at home. I've always been fiddle-footed. Guess I always will be."

He looked at Sarah Jane thoughtfully.

"Y'know, Sis, I believe you've got a wild streak in you, also, one that's just itchin' to bust out. Otherwise, you wouldn't be here with me right now. Hear me out," he said, when she started to protest. "Very few women, no matter how bad they'd been handled, would take it upon themselves to go after a band of *muy malo hombres.* Hell, I'm sorry, heck, that takes plenty of guts even for most *men,* let alone a female. In fact, most gals, unless they're ranchers' wives or daughters, won't wear men's denims, or ride astride like you are, even here in Texas. It's considered scandalous by most women, and a lot of men, too. You sit a horse like you were born to the saddle, and you wear Hank's gun as if it was made for you. So here you are with me, goin' after the men who wronged you. You're one plucky woman, Sis. And I'm proud to say that."

"Luke, you can curse in front of me," Sarah Jane said. "I grew up in a frontier town, so I've heard just about the foulest language possible. I don't exactly have virgin ears. Hank's the one who taught me how to ride so well. He said it was ridiculous that a woman had to ride sidesaddle. As far as my being here with you, I know it isn't right, but I just couldn't mope around Sonora for an entire year, wearing black and mourning, being pitied by everyone. I would have gone stir crazy."

"I can understand that. You want some more coffee?"

"Please."

When Luke got up to take Sarah Jane's mug, pain once again shot through his guts. He winced, and placed a hand to his belly.

"Little brother, whatever's wrong with you is more than just a stitch," Sarah Jane said. "Tell me what the hell is goin' on with you. And don't look so shocked about my swearing. Hank never did."

"Okay, I imagine you'd have found out sooner or later anyway," Luke said. "Soon as I fill our mugs and roll myself a smoke, I'll tell you."

He refilled both mugs, handed Sarah Jane hers, then settled alongside her and rolled a quirly. He struck a match to life on his belt buckle, then lit the smoke. After taking a long drag, he exhaled a ring of blue smoke into the gathering twilight, and sighed.

"A few weeks back, I was leadin' a patrol, searchin' for a band of outlaws, which was bossed by a man named Matt Spencer. He was one of the meanest sons of . . . bitches who ever dirtied the face of God's green Earth. We caught up with 'em in Black Seminole Canyon, just before they were able to cross the Rio Grande and escape into Mexico. They'd set an ambush for us. Luckily, one of my men, a brand new Ranger, youngster name of Joe Driscoll, spotted the trap. If he hadn't, we'd have all been shot out of our saddles before we even knew what hit us. But, since he did, we were able to turn the tables, and spring that trap. We killed every one of those *hombres*. It was a hard fight, though. Two of my men died, and two more were wounded, includin' Joe. He took a bullet in his chest, but he's gonna pull through."

"I'm sorry, Luke. But what about you?"

"We had to battle our way up a ridge where the gang was dug in. I took a bullet in my leg, then, a couple of minutes later, another one in the belly. I was still able to keep fightin', until a slug clipped my right arm, and nicked the bone. That put me down for good. By then, the fight was just about over. We picked up our dead and wounded, includin' me, and headed back to camp. Our company surgeon, Doc Mathis, was able to dig the bullet out of my belly, patch up my leg, and set my broken arm. Once I was well enough to travel, I was sent home to recuperate. That's where I was when the message about Hank's murder caught up to me. It also said you'd been hurt, but not how badly. I lit right out for Sonora as fast as I could saddle my horses."

"That means you're still hurt, and should be home in bed, recovering. Luke, what in the world is the matter with you?"

"So should you, yet here you are with me," Luke shot back.

"*Touché*," Sarah Jane said.

"Anyway, if you'll let me finish, I'm not hurtin' all that bad. I was just about ready to go back on duty anyway. My arm and leg are completely healed. The wound in my gut is also just about finished mendin'. The only time it hurts is if I twist the wrong way. Doc Patterson at home said it'll only be a couple more weeks before that pain'll stop."

"Which means you should have waited until you were completely recovered before you went back to work."

"With my brother-in-law, the man who taught me most of what I know about law work, dead, and my only sister hurt? Not a chance. You know me better'n that, Sis."

"Still, if anything happens to you . . ."

"It won't. And if it makes you feel any better, officially, I'm still on medical leave. I sent a message to Austin tellin' Headquarters what I was up to, but I didn't wait for a reply. I'm pretty certain when it came, it would have ordered me to forget about takin' after the men who'd killed Hank, that they'd have another Ranger take the assignment. I wasn't about to give them the chance to do that."

"But if you're on leave, doesn't that mean you have no authority to make an arrest?"

"Technically, mebbe. But the Rangers have never been real good at playin' strictly by the rules, not with the *hombres* we're always runnin' up against. And I'm still a commissioned officer in the outfit. You needn't worry about that. It doesn't matter anyway. Badge or not, I won't quit until I run those bastards to ground. Bet your pretty flowered and feathered hat on it."

"You should have noticed I'm not exactly wearing a lady's *chapeau*."

"I know. It was just an expression," Hank said. "Look, if you're done with your supper, I'll wash the dishes, then we should turn in. We've still got two full days of ridin' ahead of us, and I'd like to start out tomorrow mornin' as soon as there's enough daylight to see."

"I'm finished, and I'll give you a hand with the dishes," Sarah Jane answered. "We'll be done sooner that way."

"I won't turn that offer down," Luke said.

Once the dishes were done, Luke and Sarah went to make certain the horses were secured for the night. Pete and RePete, knowing Luke always had a final treat for them, paused in their grazing, lifted their heads, and whinnied. Casey whickered softly at Sarah Jane.

"Of course I've got your treats, you beggin' biscuit eaters," Luke said, chuckling. He gave each horse half of the peppermint stick that came in the package of coffee, as well as a leftover biscuit. They took the treats, then nuzzled his cheek. He kissed each one on the nose.

"Good night, you two, and get some sleep," he told them. "We've still got a ways to go. I'll see you in the mornin'. Don't let any Comanch' sneak up on us while we're sleepin'."

He gave his horses a final pat on the neck, then

joined Sarah Jane, who was stroking her horse's neck. Casey was crunching on a lemon drop she had given him, and was nosing her hip pocket, searching for another treat.

"Here, Sis. Give him this."

Luke handed Sarah Jane another leftover biscuit. Casey snatched it from her hand.

"He seems to like you well enough," Luke said.

"He does, but I believe he's missing Hank. He seems kind of sad," Sarah Jane answered.

"I'm certain he does miss Hank. They spent a lot of years, and covered a lot of miles, together. A man and horse develop a special bond, especially in our kind of work. They have to trust each other, almost like human partners, if they want to live for long. That's why I treat my horses so well, and so did Hank. Neither one of us could abide an *hombre* who'd mistreat a horse. Give Casey a little time, treat him kind, and he'll come to love you as much as he loved Hank. I guarantee it."

Sarah Jane gave Casey another lemon drop.

"If you ain't careful, Sis, you're gonna spoil that horse," Luke said. "He'll end up an incorrigible pie biter, just like my two."

"What's a pie biter, Luke?"

"Same as a biscuit eater. It's a horse who's been spoiled by his rider, and hangs around camp, beggin' for treats. Yes, I'll admit I spoil my horses. When you're alone on the trail as much as I am, and Hank was, your horse becomes your best friend. He's someone to talk to when there's no one else around to listen. And he never talks back."

"If Addie ever heard you talkin' about your horses like that, she'd be jealous," Sarah Jane said, laughing. "You might find yourself sleeping in the barn."

"She already knows," Luke answered. "She's told me, more'n once, that she can handle any woman who might try and steal me away from her, but she's not certain about my horses, or the Rangers. Then again, she understands, because she loves owning a newspaper every bit as much as I love bein' a Ranger. Say good night to Casey. It's time we get under our own blankets."

"All right. Good night, sweet boy."

Sarah Jane gave the bay a hug.

"See you in the morning, Casey. Get plenty of rest."

"He'll do more eatin' than sleepin'. That's just a horse's nature," Luke said. "But not mine. I'm plumb tuckered out."

He and his sister spread out their blankets alongside the dying campfire's embers.

"Let me know if it gets too cold for you, and I'll toss some more wood on the fire," Luke said. "Unless you get chilly, I'd rather let it die out, just in case there's anyone out here snoopin' around."

"Do you really think there might be?"

Luke shrugged.

"Probably not, but you can never be certain. One thing I do know. Most folks up and about this time of the night, way out here, are generally up to no good. The Comanches and Apaches aren't much trouble nowadays, since they've mostly been driven into Mexico. The Kiowas are mainly up on their reservation in the Territories, and the Karankawas were wiped out long ago. There might be an occasional small band of Indians prowlin' about, lookin' to raid a ranch and steal some horses, but it's mostly the white or Mexican outlaws we have to watch out for nowadays. Don't you worry, though. Just get a good night's rest. I sleep with one eye open and my gun close at hand, so I'll be ready for any trouble that might happen. The horses will also let us know if somethin', or someone, is tryin' to sneak up on us. We'll be just fine."

"I hope so. Good night, Luke."

"G'night, Sis."

After Sarah Jane was curled up under her blankets, Luke pulled off his hat, boots, and gun belt, then slid under his, keeping his six-gun alongside his right hand.

"Luke?"

"Yeah, Sis?"

"I just wanted to thank you again for understanding. I know you didn't really want me along with you."

"*Por nada.* You're right, I didn't, but since you're here, I have to admit, I'm kinda glad to have the company. As long as you listen to what I tell you, especially when we do catch up with those hombres, you'll be just fine. We both will. Now get some sleep."

Luke turned his back to Sarah Jane. Within ten minutes, they were both sleeping soundly.

The weather turned cooler the next day, which meant Luke and Sarah Jane were able to set a faster pace without exhausting the horses. They stopped for the night on the banks of the Devil's River.

"I dunno about you, but I sure could use a swim, Sis," Luke said. "You mind if I take one before I make supper?"

"Not at all. I'd certainly like to take a bath," Sarah Jane answered. "There seem to be plenty of rocks to provide enough privacy."

"All right. As soon as we care for the horses we'll clean ourselves up. It'll feel good to get some of this trail dust out of my hide. I've got a bar of Pears' soap in my saddlebags. I'll cut it in half to share with you."

"What about drying off?"

"You'll find a towel in one of your saddlebags, Sis. Or, you can just let the breeze do the job."

"The air's got a bit of a chill. I believe I'll appreciate the towel, little brother."

"Then there you go."

After getting her soap and towel, Sarah Jane walked through some brush that would screen her from Luke's view, to where the river had cut into its bank, forming a deep pool. Not that she was worried about Luke attempting to catch a glimpse of her. They hadn't seen each other unclothed since well before they were ten years old, even while growing up in a small house, where the bathtub was a zinc one dragged into the kitchen every Saturday night, with only a curtain hung for privacy. However, if he accidentally saw her in a state of undress, the bruises which still covered her body would be obvious. She had no desire to inflame his anger by allowing him to see just how badly she had been beaten. She removed her clothing, then stepped into the water, giving a sigh of pure pleasure as it began to take some of the pain from her aching leg muscles. The ride had been much harder on her than she'd let on, and she wasn't certain how much longer she would be able to hide that from Luke. Soaking in the river would certainly help, though.

Luke, for his part, went a short distance downstream, where he took off his clothes and tossed them on the bank, then plunged into the refreshing water in a long, shallow dive. After swimming across the Devil several times, he settled into a shallow spot along the riverbank, sitting where the water reached halfway up his chest. He ducked his head in the river, lathered his hair, washed it, then his face and neck. After rinsing those off, he scrubbed the rest of his body. Finally, he leaned back against an underwater rock, letting the slow current sooth the stiffness from his muscles and joints.

I still don't know if I should've let Sarah Jane come with me, he thought. *It's gonna be tough enough goin' up against a pack of killers, who've probably got most of the town on their side, without havin' to worry about my sister, too. I should've put my foot down, and made her stay back in Sonora. The last thing I need is her stumblin' into the middle of a gunfight, or gettin' so mad when she sees those hombres again she loses her head, and does somethin' stupid.*

Luke sighed, and settled more deeply into the water, until only his head was visible. He smiled to himself.

Hell, who am I kiddin'? If I'd told her to stay home, she'd have followed me anyway. There's no way I could have stopped her, short of hog-tyin' her and tossin' her in a cell. She sure can ride, and since Hank taught her to shoot, I'd bet my hat she can hit what she's aimin' at. She might be plumb handy to have sidin' me. Of course, Ma and Pa must be spinnin' in their graves, knowin' what she's up to, and that I let her. I just hope and pray we both come out of Williams City alive.

After their swims, Luke made the usual camp supper of bacon, beans, and biscuits.

"Luke, what time will we arrive in Williams City?" Sarah Jane asked, after taking a swallow of coffee.

"We should get there just around sundown, give or take," Luke answered. "Any particular reason you ask?"

"I'm just wondering how you plan on handling those men we're after."

"You mean I'm after. You're to stay out of things unless I need your help. I'm still not certain I did the right thing by lettin' you come along. But I'll let that go for now. Honestly, I'm still ponderin' on exactly what to do. First of all, they might not even be there."

"It they're not, then what?"

"Someone will be around who can tell us where to find 'em, or where they went. That means we'll have more travelin' to do. I've been thinkin' it might be best to go straight to the Rocking W Ranch. That's the most likely place for them to hole up. They probably figure no one would dare try to take 'em there. However, it might be best to go into town first, and do some nosin' around. We might find someone who doesn't care all that much for the Williamses, and would give us an idea just what we'll be up against."

"How about stopping to see the town marshal?"

Luke shook his head.

"That's what I'd usually do, stop and let the local law know there was a Ranger in town. However, in a town like Williams City, you can be certain the law is in Zach Williams's pocket. It's highly unlikely we'd get any help from the marshal, or any of his deputies. Besides, a small town like Williams City probably only has one lawman. It's not large enough to need any deputies. Most desperadoes will avoid a town controlled by one man. They'd look for easier pickin's somewhere else. We won't be able to count on any help from the county sheriff, either. The county seat's way down in Del Rio. He'd have no reason to send one of his deputies up here, unless someone sent him a complaint. I sure didn't want to waste the time it would take ridin' to Del Rio. That's not how the Rangers operate anyway. We handle things on our own, as we see fit."

"You make it sound as if we'll be on our own when we ride into town."

"We most likely will be, unless we can scare up an *hombre* who's sick and tired of bein' under Zach Williams's thumb. That ain't very likely."

"Let me see if I can help, by thinking out loud," Sarah Jane said. "If we go straight to the ranch, we'll have surprise on our side, especially if the Williams brothers and their pardners believe I'm dead, so no one has any idea where to look for Hank's killers. However, we'll also be outnumbered, which will put us at a disadvantage. That is, unless we can turn their father and the rest of their family against them. Most men will tolerate rustling, thieving, and even killing, but they won't stand for an *hombre* who mistreats a woman. Do you happen to know if their mother is still alive, or if they have any sisters? That could work to our advantage."

"Their mother died quite a few years back. Supposedly, she was trampled by a locoed bronc, but there's always been suspicions she was killed by her husband. He's got the reputation of a mean old bastard. He'd go into town and beat on . . .'"

"You can say it, Luke. He'd beat on the prostitutes."

"Yeah. Supposedly he liked to play rough. His wife had finally gotten fed up, and filed for divorce. Two weeks later, she was dead. As far as any other kids, there's just one more brother, who's still a youngster, about seventeen or eighteen."

"Which means there'll be no women to maybe listen to our story."

"Nope. Even if there were, they'd probably be too scared of Zach and his boys to do anything."

"Could we sneak onto the ranch and capture them?"

"It's possible, but risky. First, we don't know if they'll be in the house, or out on the range somewhere. Second, we wouldn't know where to find 'em in the house. Third, there's liable to be dogs that'll sound off. Fourth, it'd be almost impossible to get those boys out of the house and away from the ranch without bein' discovered. There's no way we can get in and out without makin' at least some noise, and if we were spotted someone'd be bound to raise a ruckus."

"We could just shoot our way in there, kill 'em, then shoot our way back out," Sarah Jane suggested. "It wouldn't matter to me if I were killed, as long as I knew those bastards were dead, and Hank and I were avenged."

"I can't do that. I sure don't want to get myself killed, leavin' Addie a widow and my kids fatherless. You don't really want to die, either. You might feel that way right now, but you don't. If you did, you'd have given up and died back in the doctor's office in Sonora. You're too much of a fighter, Sis. I have to give 'em a chance to surrender, and face a judge and jury. That's the oath I swore when I signed on with the Rangers. Also, the odds are only Hutch and Mace will be in the main house. The other three will be in the bunkhouse, unless they're out workin' cows. That is, if Slate Martin is even still in the territory. He's probably collected his pay, and already moved on. Getting the Williamses is only the beginning of the job. I want all five of those sons of bitches. I'm certain you do, too."

"You're right. I won't rest until they're all dead, or in jail waiting to be hung. I guess my next question is, would there be any advantage to us goin' into town first?"

"There might be, if we can find someone who'll be willing to tell us the Williamses' habits, maybe with any luck the setup of their ranch. That would be a big help. Even better would be if those boys happened to be in town. Even with the local law on their side, it'd be a lot simpler to round 'em up than havin' to try'n take 'em off their ranch. The big disadvantage would be someone might figure out what we're doin', and ride out to the Rocking W to warn 'em. That'd make chousin' those *hombres* outta there a helluva lot harder."

"It seems to me we should head into town, then."

"Right now, that's the way I'm leanin'. I'll think on it some more after I get under my blankets. We'll turn in before too long. I just need to make certain of one thing, Sis. Are you sure you want to ride in there with me? I wouldn't blame you if you didn't. In fact, it'd take a load off my mind if you hung back."

"I'm sure. And you know I am, little brother."

"I know. I just had to ask, one last time."

Chapter 12

Luke purposely waited until after dark before riding into Williams City. He and his sister slowly walked their horses down the town's sole street.

"There's the saloon up ahead, on the left. Right alongside the marshal's office. That's pretty damn convenient," Luke said. He pointed to a sign with two crossed Comanche spears at its top, with the name "The Two Spears Saloon," painted in bright red, underneath those. "A saloon's always the best place to get information in a small town. There, or the barber shop. We'll let the horses have a drink, then stop there first."

"You *are* going to let me go inside the saloon with you, aren't you, Luke?"

Luke gave a brief chuckle.

"As if I could stop you."

Sarah Jane looked around at the buildings, Luke at the passersby, as they continued down the road.

"It's pretty obvious who owns this town," Sarah Jane said. "There's the Williams Mercantile, the Williams Hotel, the Williams Weekly News, Williams Feed and Grain . . ." Her voice trailed off.

"Yeah. Now you know what we're up against,"

Luke said. "Just about everybody in town depends on Zach Williams. That means no one will back my play."

They went another hundred yards, stopped to let their horses have a short drink from the trough, then reined up in front of the harness shop, next to the saloon. After dismounting and looping their horses' reins over the hitch rail, they climbed the stairs, pushed their way through the batwing doors, and went inside the Two Spears. Most of the patrons turned to look at the new arrivals. A couple of them opened their mouths as if to speak, most likely to make some crude remark about Sarah Jane, a woman, coming into a saloon, but quickly clamped their mouths shut and returned their attention to their drinks or card games under Luke's fierce gaze.

A full figured woman in her late forties, with long brown hair and sparkling brown eyes, watched them from near the bar as they crossed the room. She was clad in an ankle length black and white dress, surprisingly for a woman working in a saloon one with a rather conservative high collar, but which showed her figure to full advantage. Despite her age and occupation, she was still quite pretty.

"Howdy, strangers," she greeted them. "Welcome to the Two Spears. My name's Eileen Willard, your hostess. What's your particular pleasure?"

"I'd like a beer to cut some of the trail dust from my throat," Luke answered. "My sister'll have a sarsaparilla. I'm Luke, she's Sarah Jane."

"I'll order those right up. I assume you'd rather have a table for you and the lady, rather'n standin' at the bar."

"You assume right, Miz Willard."

"Eileen."

"You assume right, Eileen. That empty table in the back corner will do just fine."

"Excellent. I'll bring your drinks right over."

Luke pulled out a chair for Sarah Jane, then took one for himself, where his back was to the wall, and he could see the entire room. A Ranger never kept his back to a door or window, if at all possible. To do so was just inviting an ambush bullet in the back. Sarah Jane looked around the room, taking in the mirror backed bar, the paintings of scantily clad women in various poses hanging from the walls, the gilded coal oil chandeliers, surrounded by tobacco smoke. She wrinkled her nose at the smell, a combination of sweat, spilled liquor, cheap cigars, and sawdust.

Eileen came over with their drinks. She was accompanied by another woman, a slender, short dark blonde in her early twenties.

"This is Ashlyn," she said, as she placed a mug of beer in front of Luke, an open bottle of sarsaparilla and a glass in front of Sarah Jane. "She'll be your waitress for tonight. If there's anything you need, just let her know."

"Of course. We're pleased to meet you, Ashlyn," Luke said. "Is there any chance you can rustle us up some grub?"

"I'll talk to Joe," Ashlyn answered. "He can usually fry some ham, eggs, and potatoes."

"That'll be just fine. We're obliged."

"I'll put your order in right now," Ashlyn said, with a musical laugh.

"I have to admit I'm curious," Eileen said, once Ashlyn was out of earshot. "You seem like nice folks. Most respectable women wouldn't set foot inside a place like this."

"Who says I'm a respectable woman?" Sarah Jane said. Luke glared at her.

"Don't listen to Sarah Jane," he said. "She really is a decent lady. I just couldn't bring myself to let her alone on the street, while I had a few beers. Some of the men out there seem like mighty unsavory characters. I figure she's safer in here than out there."

"Your instincts are probably right," Eileen agreed. "I've got to get back to work. Let me know if you need anythin' Ashlyn can't help you with."

"Will do," Luke said. He leaned back in his chair, took his sack of Bull Durham and cigarette papers from his vest pocket, and began rolling a smoke.

"Luke, when are we gonna start looking for the Williams brothers?" Sarah Jane asked.

"Easy, Sis. Keep your voice down. We don't want anyone overhearin' why we're in town, until I'm ready. Just be patient, and let me do things my way. It'll pay off, trust me. Besides, I always work better on a full belly. Once we're done with supper, it'll be time to get to work. Meantime, I could use another beer."

He emptied the contents of his glass, then signaled to Ashlyn.

They ate a leisurely supper, Luke having two more helpings of ham and eggs, both he and his sister requesting a slice of dried apple pie for dessert. Just before they finished their meal, Eileen returned to their table. This time, there was another woman with her.

"Luke, Sarah Jane, this is Patty Spears," Eileen said. "She and her husband Joe own this place."

"Which would explain the name of this here saloon," Luke said, with a grin. "Howdy, ma'am. You've got a nice place here. Not quite as rowdy as most saloons."

"Thanks. We try to keep it that way," Patty said. She was in her mid to late fifties, short and full figured, with graying hair cut shoulder length, her eyes hidden behind a pair of tinted spectacles. "I just wanted to make certain everythin' was satisfactory tonight. I don't like seein' any of my customers leave unhappy."

"Everythin' was just fine," Luke said. "The beer was good, and the food tasty."

"Your cook did a fine job," Sarah Jane added. "I was starved, but the meal filled me right up. Tell him I said thanks."

"He's my husband, Joe. I'll tell him. He'll be pleased to hear that," Patty answered. "Would you like anythin' else? Another drink, or perhaps some coffee?"

"No thank you," Luke answered, patting his stomach. "My belly would bust if I took another bite. Mebbe you could help us with somethin' else, though."

"Just what might that be?"

"Directions to the Rocking W Ranch."

Patty and Eileen both visibly stiffened. Patty's voice became gruff.

"Exactly what kind of business would you have with Zach Williams?"

Luke gave her a thin smile.

"Not Zach. His boys, Hutch and Mason."

"It don't matter which of the Williams you want to see," Patty snapped. "You've got to have a good reason."

"We do," Luke said. "Sarah Jane made their acquaintance a few weeks back, over Sonora way. She was really impressed with 'em, especially Hutch. He seemed pretty taken with her, too. Told her to look him up if she was ever down this way. It turns out I've got to go down to La Potasa, in Mexico, to buy some blooded bulls to improve my herd. Once Sarah Jane heard that, she pleaded with me to bring her along. I was reluctant, but since I had to pass through here on my way to Coahuila anyway, I finally gave in. You know how a woman can wear you down, 'specially one who thinks she's in love."

"I'm not certain," Patty said. "The Williams are mighty particular about visitors."

"Oh, please, Mrs. Spears, I just want to see Hutch again," Sarah Jane said. "What harm can it do, seeing him one more time? If he doesn't want to see me, Luke and I will just leave, I promise. But I have to see Hutch at least once more. You can understand why. You must have been in love once."

"I still am, with Joe, even after all these years."

"See?"

"I'm still not certain. What do you think, Eileen?"

"You know what I think about Zach Williams and his boys," Eileen answered, the tone in her voice making her hatred for them plain. "But if this young lady is bound and determined to see Hutch again, I say let her go ahead. It's not up to us to wet nurse her anyway."

"I appreciate that, Eileen," Sarah Jane said.

"You may regret it," Eileen answered.

"I guess it'll be all right, then," Patty said. "I'll

get Joe. He's much better at givin' directions than I am."

"We're obliged," Luke said.

Just then, three young cowboys burst through the door of the saloon, obviously already drunk. They began shouting for whiskey before they were halfway to the bar. Sarah Jane gasped, and stared at them in horror.

"Luke, that's one of them," she said, her hand trembling when she pointed at the man on the right. "That's the one they called Brian, the fat one there."

"Are you certain?"

"There's no way in Hell I'd ever forget any of those men. That's him."

"You stay put, Sis."

Luke got to his feet and turned to face the new arrivals.

"Hold it right there, boys," he said. His voice was low and deadly, his right hand hovering over the butt of his Peacemaker.

"Who you talkin' to, Mister? And just who in hell do you think you are?" the man in the middle challenged.

"Name's Luke Caldwell. I'm a Texas Ranger. The lady with me is my sister. Your partner should remember her. He was one of the men who killed her husband, then raped her and left her for dead, up in Sonora. I'm here to take him in. Him, and the others who were with him."

"You're plumb loco, Mister," Bryan shouted. "I've never seen that woman in my life. In fact, I've never even been to Sonora. I doubt that's your sister, either. She's just a damn whore travelin' with you, tryin' to stir up trouble for some reason. No one I know would allow his sister to walk into a saloon."

"Your name Brian?"

"It is. Dale Bryan. But that's none of your business. Mebbe you don't know it, but I work for the Rocking W. Zach Williams, who owns the ranch, and this town, won't take kindly to you claimin' I'm a killer, and violate women besides. If I were you, I'd take that damn little *puta* and leave town, right now, before you catch a bellyful of lead."

"You heard him, Sis. What do you say? Is that one of the men who killed Hank?"

Sarah Jane had come to her feet.

"Absolutely. He's lying when he says he isn't. If you make him drop his britches, I can positively identify him."

"What the hell are you talkin' about, bitch?" Bryan screamed.

"Because I'll never forget how sickening it felt when you were on top of me," Sarah Jane answered, her voice surprisingly calm. "You're a fat, filthy pig. But for a man your size, you're small where it counts the most. You have *cojones pequenas, hombre. Una gran barriga, pero cojones muy pequenas.*"

Bryan's companions burst into laughter.

"You hear what she said, Dale?" one of them asked. "She said you've got a big belly, but small balls."

"I heard what she said plain enough. And it's the last thing she'll ever say," Bryan roared, out of control with anger.

"Don't go for that gun," Luke warned. "Dale Bryan, you're under arrest for murder, attempted murder, and assault. You other two men can walk away with no problem if y'all stay out of this."

"Go ahead, Dale. We'll back your play," one of his partners said. "Ain't no female can just sashay into Williams City and insult a Rocking W hand. Besides, there's three of us, and only one of him."

"Big mistake," Luke said.

"I don't think so," Bryan snapped. He grabbed for his six-gun.

The Two Spears erupted in gunfire and powder smoke. Luke pulled his Colt smoothly from its holster. The center cowboy had just cleared leather when Luke put a bullet in his chest, dropping him in his tracks. Luke shifted his gun to the left, just as that man got his own gun level and thumbed back the hammer. Luke's bullet took the cowboy just below his breastbone. As the man stumbled, Luke shot him again. The dying cowboy squeezed the trigger of his pistol, sending a wild shot into the ceiling, then crumpled to the floor.

Luke turned to aim at Bryan, who was the slowest of the three. To his surprise, the fat cowboy had dropped his unfired gun, and was staring in disbelief at the blood spreading around a bullet hole in the middle of his belly. Sarah Jane still held her smoking pistol leveled at him.

"I guess you and your friends didn't notice there were two of us, not just one," she told Bryan. "You probably figured a dumb female wouldn't know how to draw and shoot. Let me clue you in. My brother is a Texas Ranger, and my husband was a former Ranger, then a town marshal. Do you think either of them *wouldn't* teach me how to use a gun?"

"You, you gut shot me, damn you," Bryan muttered.

"That big belly was my easiest shot. I could hardly miss it," Sarah Jane answered. "I sure couldn't aim for your *cojones*. They'd be too small a target to hit."

"I ain't dead yet."

Bryan attempted to reach his gun. Sarah Jane shot him right between the eyes, then laughed bitterly as he fell.

"Go to Hell, you rotten son of a bitch."

A shotgun's deep throated roar echoed through the saloon. Splinters rained down from the hole its charge of buckshot blasted through the ceiling.

"That's enough!" Patty shouted. "The next man who makes a move gets the other barrel, plumb center."

"And I've got two more barrels primed and ready to let loose," Joe added, from where he stood in the kitchen door, also holding a shotgun.

"It's all over, unless someone else wants to take a hand," Luke said. "Any more of you *hombres* want to die today? I promise you it won't be me or my sister who does."

He was answered with dead silence. A few men shook their heads.

"Patty, you'd better send someone for the marshal," Luke ordered. He fumbled in his shirt pocket for his badge, then pinned the silver star on silver circle to his vest.

Ashlyn was staring in shock at the dead men.

"Ashlyn, go find the marshal," Patty told her. "He's probably at the café, havin' a late supper."

"If he heard the gunfire, he's already on his way," Ashlyn answered.

"You just go and make certain he is, girl."

"Yes'm," Ashlyn mumbled. She scurried out the door.

"The rest of you can go back to your drinkin' or gambling, but make certain you keep your hands where I can see 'em, and away from your guns," Luke said. "Nobody leaves this place until I say so, *comprende*? Sarah Jane, keep 'em covered, while I reload, and check these *hombres* to make certain they're done for. If anyone even twitches the wrong way, plug him."

"With pleasure, little brother."

Luke punched the empties from the cylinder of his Colt, replacing the spent shells with fresh ones. He checked Bryan and his partners, who had indeed breathed their last, their blood soaking into the sawdust covering the floor. He'd no sooner done this when the marshal burst through the doors, holding a sawed-off Greener in his hands.

"What the devil's goin' on here?" he shouted. "Who started all this?"

"Luke. It's him!" Sarah Jane screamed, her voice shaking. "That's the man they called Slate."

Luke found himself looking into the most evil eyes he'd ever seen, the yellowish brown eyes of a born killer. Behind those eyes was a sallow face, with a ginger colored moustache gracing its upper lip. And that face was framed by a tangle of shoulder length, reddish blond hair. A good sized chunk of hair was missing from over the marshal's right ear.

"What the hell is she talkin' about? And who started all the shootin'?" Martin yelled.

"He did," Luke answered, pointing to Dale Bryan's body. "When I tried to arrest him, he objected. I warned him and his pards not to go for their guns, but they did anyway. Stupid of them."

"Why were you tryin' to arrest 'em, Ranger? And how does that gal know my name?"

"You don't recognize her, Marshal?"

"No. Should I?"

"I believe you should. Perhaps this will help jog your memory."

Luke reached into his right shirt pocket and pulled out the hank of hair which had been found in Sarah Jane's hand.

"By any chance are you missin' this, Marshal? It seems to match yours."

"What the hell? It's you!" Martin screamed, as he recognized Sarah Jane. "You should be dead, along with your damned husband."

"You made a mistake by not finishin' the job," Sarah Jane answered. "You killed my husband, and ruined my life. Now you're gonna pay for it."

"I have no idea what you're talkin' about," Martin said, trying to stall for time.

"Funny, you just said you did, Marshal," Luke said. "You can tell your story to a judge and jury. Somehow I don't think they'll buy it. Now drop that scattergun, then unbuckle your gun belt and drop it, too. Otherwise, I'll let my sister put so many holes in you the Spears will be able to use you for a sieve. Your choice. Leave town in handcuffs, or draped belly down over the saddle of your horse."

"That woman's your sister?"

"That's right."

"But she's insane."

"Right again. So, what's it gonna be?"

"There's no possible way you can make those charges stick, Ranger. I'll go along peaceably."

"That's smart. Now drop the guns."

Martin placed the shotgun on the floor, then started to unbuckle his gun belt. Ashlyn came through the door, short of breath.

"I couldn't find the marshal," she gasped.

"I'm right here, honey," Martin said. He grabbed Ashlyn, and wrapped his arm around her throat, cutting off her breath. He pulled his .44 Smith and Wesson from its holster and pressed the barrel to Ashlyn's temple.

"Now, Ranger, *you* lower the guns, you and your sister both, or I'll blow this little girl's brains out. Do it!" he snapped, when Luke hesitated.

"I reckon I've got no choice. Do what the man says, Sarah Jane," Luke said. He lowered his pistol, then let it drop to the floor.

"This time I'm gonna make certain you're dead, lady, then I'm gonna finish off your brother," Martin said, with a sneer. He took his gun away from Ashlyn's temple, to aim at Sarah Jane's chest. When he did, Ashlyn kicked him in the shin. At the same time, a small caliber pistol popped twice. Martin flinched in pain, a trickle of blood appeared at the corner of his mouth. He loosened his grip on the girl.

"Get down, Ashlyn!" Luke shouted, as he dove to his belly and grabbed his gun. He slammed two bullets into Martin's chest. Sarah Jane, fury at the man who had mistreated her so badly replacing her fear, put three bullets into Martin's belly. Martin's knees buckled, then he fell face down, revealing two bullet holes high in his back. Behind him stood Eileen, holding a two shot Derringer. Smoke still trailed from the deadly little gun's barrel. She hurried up to Ashlyn, and knelt alongside her.

"Are you all right, honey?" she asked.

"I . . . I think so," Ashlyn answered.

"You were very brave, especially when you kicked the marshal in his shin," Eileen said.

Luke used the toe of his boot to roll Martin onto his back.

"Is he dead?" Sarah Jane asked.

"He damn for certain is," Luke answered. "I'd imagine he's shakin' hands with the Devil right about now. How about you, Sis?"

"I'm just fine."

"You handled yourself real well. I don't know if I could've downed all those first three *hombres* without your help."

Eileen had gotten to her feet, and was hugging Ashlyn. Patty and Joe were with them.

"Eileen, you probably saved all our lives," Luke said. "We're obliged. You were a big help too, Ashlyn. Joe and Patty, thanks for backin' us up. The rest of you, clear on out. A few of you get the undertaker. Have him haul these bodies away."

"This town doesn't have an undertaker. I'm Steve Borden, owner of the hardware store. I handle the buryin's around here," one of the customers said.

"Then I'd say you've had a profitable night," Luke said.

"So it seems," Borden answered. "Jordan, Myers, Harley, help me drag these bodies onto the sidewalk. I'll get my buckboard and haul 'em down to my shop. I'll build the coffins tonight, and we can plant these men first thing in the mornin', unless Mr. Williams has any objections."

"I can promise you he won't," Luke said.

"Ranger, what exactly was this all about?" Eileen asked.

"Slate Martin and Dale Bryan were two of the men who killed my sister's husband, Hank Brundage, Sonora's town marshal," Luke explained. "They weren't satisfied with just that, though. They also raped Sarah Jane, and beat her almost to death. When I told her I was goin' after the bunch, she insisted on comin' with me. I can't really blame her."

"It must be a relief knowing two of them are dead," Patty said to Sarah Jane.

"It is, but I won't be able to rest until the others

238

are behind bars, or dead and buried," Sarah Jane answered.

"Which means we've got to get goin'," Luke said. "Someone's bound to get word to Zach Williams. We need to reach his place before they do. Joe, I'm appointin' you actin' town marshal. Do you mind finishin' up here?"

"No, but Zach Williams will never stand for me takin' the marshal's job. Me'n Patty don't exactly see eye to eye with him."

"You let me handle Williams. He just might find himself behind bars before this night is out. Y'see his sons, Hutch and Mace, along with an *hombre* named Jody, who I'd imagine works for Williams, are the other three men we're after. Patty, I know this is unusual, but would you and Eileen mind bein' Joe's deputies until a permanent marshal is appointed?"

"I'd be more than happy to," Patty said. "There's a few more *hombres* in this town who need straightenin' out. I'm the woman to do just that."

"Same here," Eileen said. "I'm gonna take Ashlyn home, then I'll come back. Anybody else starts trouble I'll be ready for him."

"We'll be gone by then," Luke said. "I've just got one question for you."

"What's that?"

"Where in blue blazes did you have that Derringer hidden? You couldn't have gotten it out from under your dress that quick."

"Are you kiddin' me, Ranger? I keep that gun in my built-in holster."

Eileen laughed, and glanced at her cleavage.

"Plenty of room down there."

"I'm not sayin' a word," Luke said, shaking his head. "Look, me'n Sarah Jane have got to get movin'. We'll stop back after our business is finished. We just need the way to the Rocking W."

"It's not far," Joe said. "Take the trail southeast out of town. After about a mile, you'll see a fork to the right, headin' east. That's the road to the Williams spread. It's about two miles from the junction. But you'd best be careful. Zach runs a tough crew."

"We will be," Luke assured him. "*Adios.*"

"*Adios.*"

Chapter 13

Luke kept the horses at a hard gallop until they reached the turnoff for the Rocking W, then slowed to a fast walk.

"Why are we slowing down?" Sarah Jane asked.

"A couple of reasons. First, we don't want to wear out the horses, on the chance we'll need 'em as fresh as possible if we get involved in a chase. They haven't had much rest since we left Sonora, so we've got to conserve their energy. Second, since this road ends at the Williams place, anyone leavin' there can't get past without us seein' 'em. Third, we want to ride up to the house as quietly as possible, so I can get a chance to look things over before we ride on in. I know you're impatient, Sis. So am I. But it's better to take our time to be certain what we're up against, rather'n blunderin' into a trap that'll get us killed. Takin' that extra bit of time just might be the difference between livin' and dyin'. It's just like in a gunfight. It ain't necessarily the man who pulls faster and shoots first. It's the *hombre* who takes the extra split-second to aim carefully who's usually still standin' when the smoke clears."

"Do you think anyone was able to ride ahead and warn the Williamses we're comin'?"

"I doubt it. The moon's nearly full, so it's almost as bright as daylight out here. I haven't seen any riders toppin' the rises ahead of us. There's no fresh hoof prints in the road, and no dust risin'. I can't smell any dust on the air, either. I'd say the Williams boys won't be expectin' company."

"But with the bright moon, anyone watching will see us ride in," Sarah Jane pointed out.

Luke grinned.

"Now you're talkin' like a lawman, Sis. And I ain't worried about you handlin' a gun anymore, neither. Not after you plugged that *hombre* dead center back in Sonora. I wasn't certain you'd have the nerve. You sure proved me wrong."

"That would be a law *woman,* little brother," Sarah Jane retorted. "And I generally hit what I'm aimin' at. Of course, I could hardly miss that big gut. And it was a helluva good feeling putting those bullets into that fat bastard after what he did to me."

Luke shook his head and grinned again.

"Says the woman who just claimed to be a respectable lady."

"A respectable lady who won't be pushed around by any man. Not ever again."

This time, Luke laughed.

"I reckon you're right, at that. All right, no more talkin'. We can't risk bein' overheard."

Luke slowed the pace even more. Forty minutes later, they reached the Rocking W. The entrance was marked with an arched wrought iron sign of the ranch name, and its brand.

Luke held up his hand and reined in Pete.

"Hold up, Sis. Let's get off the trail and into the brush while I size up the situation."

He turned Pete, with RePete following, into a gap in the mesquite and greasewood. Once Sarah Jane had Casey out of sight of the ranch house, Luke pulled his horses to a halt, where the brush was high enough to offer good concealment, but still low enough he could see the ranch buildings. He reached into his saddlebag, pulled out his field glasses, and placed them to his eyes, using the brim of his hat to shield the lenses from the moonlight, which might glint off the glass and be seen by anyone in the main house. He spent several minutes scanning the ranch, studying the buildings carefully. Finally, he lowered the glasses.

"What do you think, Luke?"

"I'm not certain. There's no lights in the bunkhouse. That means either the hands are asleep, or most of 'em are out on the range, tendin' to the cows. That's pretty unlikely, unless Williams is worried about rustlers. I doubt that, though. Mebbe a small rancher or farmer might take a beef or two, but they'd be takin' a long chance. So would any roamin' band of cow thieves. A man like Zach Williams'll run a rough outfit. He'd hang anyone he suspected of rustlin', without a trial. A man'd have to be awful salty to try'n steal any Rocking W cows."

"What about the main house? There seem to be plenty of lights on."

"I was wonderin' about that, too. It might just be that Zach and his boys are up late, mebbe goin' over the books, tryin' to figure out where to get the best price for their beef, or just palaverin' before turnin' in."

"So what do we do? It would have been better if everyone was asleep. Then we could have gotten into the house before anyone realized we were there. We'd have caught those men asleep, and captured them without too much trouble. Am I right, Luke?"

"Mebbe, mebbe not. If there's any dogs about the place, and there probably are, they'd start barkin' a warning. The main problem, though, would be finding the bedrooms before we were discovered. It'd be pretty difficult to locate the right rooms in a house that big."

The Rocking W's main house was a low, sprawling adobe structure, with a veranda running across its entire façade.

"So our best hope is the entire family is in one room."

"Right again, Sis. We're gonna head down there nice and quiet-like, and knock on the door. Luckily, those thick adobe walls will muffle whatever sound we might make. Soon as that door's opened, whoever's behind it will be staring right down our gun barrels. You ready?"

"I've been ready since that awful day."

"Good. No point in puttin' this off. Let's head on down there. Mebbe they'll offer us tea and crumpets . . . but I doubt it."

Luke and Sarah Jane rode down the slope and into the yard, dismounting and ground-tying their horses underneath the shelter of a large cottonwood tree.

"You two keep quiet," Luke warned Pete and RePete, with a pat to their noses and a piece of licorice.

"That goes for you too, Casey," Sarah Jane said. She gave the gelding a lemon drop. He took it, then nuzzled her shoulder.

"Let's go, Sis," Luke whispered. "Follow my lead."

Keeping low, guns at the ready, they crossed the yard and stepped onto the veranda. Luke stood at one side of the door, and waved Sarah Jane to the other. He rapped on the heavy oak with the barrel of his pistol. A rustle of movement came from inside. A moment later, the door was flung open. A young man, who bore a striking resemblance to Hutch and Mason Williams, stood there, the color draining from his face when he found himself looking down the barrels of two .45 Colts, pointed straight at his chest.

"Raise your hands," Luke ordered. The man

hesitated, looked at the badge pinned to Luke's vest, then complied. He raised his hands shoulder high.

"Who's at the door, Mitch?" asked a voice from the parlor.

Mitch looked questioningly at Luke.

"Go ahead, tell him."

"It's a Texas Ranger and some woman, Pa."

"I'll be right there."

Zachary Williams came into the hall, carrying a double-barreled Remington shotgun. Its hammers were already cocked.

"Lower the hammers and drop the gun, Mr. Williams," Luke ordered. "I won't ask twice. Once you do, shuck the gun belt, too. We're not lookin' for trouble here."

Luke waggled his Peacemaker for emphasis.

Williams glared at Luke, but he eased off the shotgun's triggers, carefully lowered the hammers, then placed the gun on the floor.

"Now the gun belt," Luke said. "One-handed."

Using his left hand, Williams unbuckled his gun belt, and let it drop to his ankles. He began cursing at his son.

"Mitch, how the hell many times have I told you never to answer the damn door without a gun in your hand? And where the hell is the damn dog?"

"How should I know? Probably runnin' off a coyote," Mitch answered.

"That's enough, Williams," Luke snapped. "I'm lookin' for your other two boys, Hutch and Mace. I'm also lookin' for a cowboy named Jody. They here?"

"No, they ain't. Why're you lookin' for 'em?"

"They're suspects in the murder of the town marshal, up in Sonora. They're also accused of beating and raping his wife."

"That's a damn lie. Couldn't have been my boys. They've been right here on the ranch until just a couple of days ago. Who made up those wild claims, Ranger?"

"I did," Sarah Jane said. "I'll never forget the day your sons, and their partners, killed my husband and attacked me."

"You?" Williams spat between Sarah Jane's feet. "Why would my boys bother to have their way with you, when they could find a better lookin' two dollar whore in any sportin' house?"

"Easy, Sis," Luke said, when she eased back the hammer of her six-gun, ready to gun down Williams where he stood. "Williams, I've got more'n enough evidence to bring your boys in. And yes, this is my sister. That means the man they killed was my brother-in-law. Hank was also my ridin' pard, and a friend. Now, are you gonna tell me where they went, or do I let Sarah Jane start shootin' it outta you, one bullet at a time? If you haven't told me by the time she's done with you, I'll tear this place down, piece by piece, to make certain they aren't hidin' somewhere on this property."

"Ranger, you'd better get outta here, right now. If you do, you just might save your job."

"Not a chance."

"Mitch, go for the marshal," Williams ordered.

"But Pa. They'll shoot me."

"They ain't gonna shoot you, dammit. You're just a kid, who hasn't done nothin'. Do what I say and go for the marshal."

"Pa . . ."

"Go, you snivelin', yellow-bellied coward."

"Let me handle this, son," Luke said. "Williams, first, I don't want to shoot your boy, but I sure as hell will stop him from tryin' to leave this house. Goin' for the marshal won't do you any good anyhow. He's dead. So are three of your hands, includin' Dale Bryan. You see, him and Slate Martin were two of the men with your sons when they killed Hank and attacked my sister. I reckon they thought she was dead, so no one'd ever know who committed the killings. We ran into Bryan and his pards at one of the saloons in town. When we tried to arrest Bryan, he and his pals decided to shoot it out with us. That didn't turn out so well, for them. When Slate Martin came into the saloon, we tried to arrest *him*. He grabbed one of the bar girls and threatened to kill her. One of the other gals shot him in the back, then me'n my sister finished him off. You'll be lucky if I don't arrest you for hirin' an *hombre* like Martin to run things in your town. Now, are you gonna tell me where your other two boys are, or do I turn my sister loose on you?"

Williams shrugged.

"Damn you and your sister to Hell, Ranger. But I reckon it won't do no harm to tell you, since you can't touch them where they're at anyway. I've got another spread, down in Mexico. Some of the peons have been tryin' to squat on my land. I told Hutch and Mace to take some of the boys down there and take care of the problem. Jody went with them. They were safe from any Texas lawman once they crossed the Rio Grande."

"Where exactly in Mexico?"

"Why the hell do you think I'd tell you that, Ranger? Besides, you've got no authority down there. None. *Nada*. So try'n find my boys. You never will. And you can be damn certain if you do, they'll kill you."

"Since when has the Rio Grande ever stopped the Rangers?" Luke shot back. "I don't imagine it'll be too hard to figure out where your spread is at. I've got some friends in the *Rurales*. I'd imagine they would be more than happy to take some *Yanqui gringo* sons of bitches into custody, who've been killin' the locals. In fact, it'd give me real pleasure to know your boys are rottin' in a Mexican prison, waitin' for the firin' squad. You know how things work below the Border.

Guilty until proven innocent. You can bet your sombrero me'n Sarah Jane will make certain the Mexican authorities know your boys are guilty as sin."

"You can't buck me and get away with it. I've got too much influence, even in Austin."

"That won't do you much good if you're dead, Williams."

"Pa, that's enough," Mitch said. "You always said I was like Ma, that I was no good for nothin'. You always favored Hutch and Mitch over me, simply 'cause they're always ready to run over anyone who gets in their way, just like you. You've got more'n enough land and money, yet you always want more. Now see where it's got you. Take a good look at that gal's face. You can still see the bruises, and the scars. She'll have some of those the rest of her life. Is that what you wanted, to raise sons who murder lawmen, poor farmers and Mexican peasants? Then, to top it off, they violate innocent women. Well, dammit, I'm puttin' a stop to it, right here and now. Ma'am, was it really my brothers who did that to you?"

"Yes."

"I'll tell you where to find them. The ranch is . . ."

"Mitch, shut up, you little bastard."

"You'd know more about that than I would, *Father!*"

"I mean it, Mitch. Shut the hell up. You're just like your Ma was, weak. You've always been a disappointment to me."

"No, Pa. I'm through bein' kept under your thumb. I'm finally found the guts to stand up to you. You're not gonna do to me what you did to Ma, browbeat her until you crushed her spirit. Then you killed her."

"That's not so. She was trampled by a locoed mustang. And this is one helluva time for you to find your backbone. You're gonna be sorry, boy."

"I doubt it. You see, even if you kill me, Pa, I'll die with my self-respect. That's somethin' you wouldn't know about. Ranger, our Mexico ranch is about thirty miles due south of here, about two miles beyond the Rio. It won't be easy roustin' my brothers out of there. They took all of Pa's hired guns along. You might be interested to know the place is used to move wet cows, too, in both directions across the Border."

"I warned you to keep your damn mouth shut, boy. Now I'm gonna have to shut it for you."

Williams dove for his pistol, kicking Mitch's feet out from under him as he did. Both of them scrambled for the gun. Mitch reached it first, but before he could roll over and toss it out of reach, his father grabbed his wrist, slammed it against the floor, and wrested the gun from his son's grasp. He twisted, getting off one wild shot, which punched a hole in the ceiling, before Mitch was able to jump atop him, forcing his arm down.

Luke was unable to take a shot while the Williamses wrestled for control of the gun, fearful his bullet would strike Mitch, instead of his father.

"Luke, can't you do something?" Sarah Jane cried.

"Not without mebbe killin' the youngster," Luke said. "I can't chance it."

Williams had scrambled atop Mitch, pressing the gun against his son's stomach. Mitch was unable to fight his father off, writhing to try and avoid the bullet he knew was coming. He managed to wrap his hand around his father's wrist. The gun went off with a muffled bang. Mitch jerked, tried to rise, then sagged. His father half rose, then fell onto his side, and rolled onto his back. A crimson stain was spreading over his shirt, just above his belt buckle. The gun was still clenched in his hand. Mitch slowly stood up, shaking his strained wrist. He looked down at his father, no expression on his face.

"You . . . killed me . . . Mitch," Williams said, gasping for breath. "Never figured . . . you'd have the . . . guts to do it, boy. Thought you were . . . too much . . . like your mother."

Mitch shook his head.

"No, Pa. I didn't kill you. You died a long time ago. So did Hutch and Mace. Money, greed, and the lust for power took your lives. Y'all just were too blind to see it. You didn't care who you hurt, Ma included. It took more guts for me to not fall into bein' like you, than it took to put a bullet in you."

"Damn you. I'll take you to Hell with me."

Williams struggled to raise his gun. Mitch pulled it from his hand, and tossed it at Luke's feet.

"Mebbe Hutch or Mace will, but not you, Pa. Not today."

Whatever Williams intended to say was choked off by the blood filling his throat, and welling from his mouth. He gurgled, gave a long sigh, shuddered, then went slack.

"Mitch, are you all right?" Luke asked.

"I am. I know I should feel somethin', but I don't. I don't feel a damn thing. Any feelin's I had for my father and brothers died the same day my mother did."

"Luke, there's some men coming from the bunkhouse," Sarah Jane warned. "They must have heard the shot."

"I'll calm 'em down, Ranger, if it's all right with you," Mitch said. "You mind if I pick up Pa's gun?"

"Go ahead, but remember I'm keeping my gun ready. First man who makes a wrong move will catch a bullet. That includes you."

"I understand."

Four men, who'd been roused from their sleep,

then hurriedly pulled on their boots and grabbed their guns, came into the house. Mitch and Luke, both with their six-guns leveled, met them just inside the door.

"Mitch, we heard a shot," the lead man said. "What the hell's goin' on? And what the hell are the Rangers doin' here? Who's the woman?"

"Shep, listen close, all of you," Mitch answered. "My father's dead."

"This damned Ranger killed him?" Shep exclaimed.

"No, he didn't. I did."

"*You* killed your pa? That makes no sense. Why? We all knew you'n him didn't see things eye to eye, but why'd you kill him?"

"Because he tried to kill me."

"Huh?"

"This Ranger came lookin' for Hutch and Mace. Pa wouldn't tell him where to find 'em, so I did. That's when Pa tried to kill me."

"Mitch, let me take over," Luke said.

"Mebbe you'd better, Ranger. This is the ranch foreman, Shep Mittler, and most of the hands that are still here, except for the ones that went to Mexico with my brothers. The rest are out on the range, searchin' out strays. Those men'll be at the line shack in Doolittle Canyon, if you need to talk with 'em."

"All right. To answer your last question, Mr. Mittler, the woman with me is my sister. Hutch and Mace Williams are wanted for killing her husband, the town marshal in Sonora, then raping her and beating her almost to death. We came here lookin' for 'em. If Mister Williams had cooperated with me, none of this would have happened. He'd still be alive. Now, me'n my sister are goin' down to the Williamses' Mexican spread, to bring those two sons of bitches back to stand trial. If any of you get any fancy notions of tryin' to stop us, you'll end up like Zach Williams. That's a promise."

"Shep, I own this ranch now," Mitch said.

"Along with your brothers," Mittler answered.

"Not once they're both stretchin' a rope. Not one person who works on this ranch is to interfere with the Ranger. Anyone who tries it is fired, *comprende*? Unless I shoot 'em first."

"You made it clear."

"Mitch . . ." Luke started to say.

"Give me another minute, Ranger. Shep, it's up to you and the rest of the men to decide whether you want to stay on, workin' for me. Those who do will get five dollars a month more. Those who don't can leave with no hard feelin's."

"That's fair," Mittler answered. "I reckon we'll stay on, at least for a spell."

"Good. I'm obliged. The first order I have is for a couple of you to get my Pa's body outta the house. You can wrap it in the rug he's lyin' on. It's blood-soaked and ruined anyway. Bury him soon as it's first light. I don't care where you plant him, as long it ain't anywhere near my mother. Somewhere a mile or two off in the brush'll do just fine. After that, I'll need someone to ride out and let the rest of the men know things have changed. Then, I'll want every cow on this ranch checked. Any of 'em which are wearin' brands that appear to be blotted out or changed I want held aside, until I get back. Once I do, we'll get as many of 'em as we can back to their rightful owners. The Rocking W is gonna be an honest operation from here on out."

"What do ya mean, Mitch, until you get back? Where the hell are you goin'?"

"As long as the Ranger agrees, I'm goin' with him and his sister, to lead 'em to Hutch and Mace. Ranger?"

"Why would you want to do that, Mitch?" Luke asked. "Are you certain?"

"Yeah, Ranger, I am. Think about it. I know exactly how to get to our ranch. You don't, and even with good directions it's not all that easy to find. I can take you straight to the place. Second, they've never seen you, right?"

"No, they haven't."

"That means I can get you inside without my brothers becomin' suspicious. I'll claim you're a new gunhand my pa hired, and he had me bring you down south. You might even be able to take them into custody without havin' to fire a shot."

Luke rubbed his jaw before answering.

"It might work."

"What about me? They've damn sure seen me," Sarah Jane asked.

"You can keep your hat pulled low, with your hair tucked up under it," Mitch said. "You're wearin' men's pants, and a man's shirt. Smear some dirt on your face, and no one'd recognize you as a woman, leastwise not right off. So what do you say, Ranger?"

"It's a helluva lot better idea than just tryin' to sneak in there and catch your brothers and their friends by surprise, or attemptin' to shoot our way onto the place," Luke said. "Only thing is those gunfighters you said went down to Mexico with your brothers. I doubt they'll let us just waltz in there, arrest Hutch and Mace, and then just sashay out of there, pretty as you please. And there's always the chance me and one or more of 'em have crossed paths before."

"Another reason you need me along. I'm pretty handy with a gun. Seems to me you could use an extra one."

"Luke, he could be leadin' us into a trap," Sarah Jane pointed out.

"I know that, Sis. It's a long chance we're takin', no matter how we handle the situation. My gut tells me we can trust him. But Mitch, I'm warning you, if you are leadin' us into a dry-gulchin', you'll catch the first bullets. Unless

257

you've got any proof you're on the level. If you and your pa hated each other as much as you say, he just might've cut you out of his will. That'd be a powerful motive for murder."

"Why? Do you think this is some elaborate scheme I have to get rid of my whole family, so I inherit all my father's property? I didn't even know you were gonna show up here tonight, Ranger. I'd have to think awful fast to come up with a plan like that, even if I'd ever had such a thought, which I ain't. All I can give you is my word I ain't lyin' to you."

"I can vouch for Mitch, Ranger," Mittler said. "He's never wanted nothin' but to be left alone, workin' with the horse wranglers. There's not a dishonest bone in the boy's body. He couldn't bring himself to tell a lie even if an *hombre* was holdin' a .44 Colt stuck in his belly, with the hammer cocked and ready to go off. He's like his ma was, that way."

"All right, I'll take a chance on you, Mitch," Luke said. "Once this is over, assuming we all come back alive, I won't press rustlin' charges against you or any of the men here, as long as you stick to what you just said, and make certain any stolen cows get back to their owners. Agreed?"

"Agreed."

"What about the rest of you boys?"

Mittler looked at the other men, who nodded their agreement.

"That's more'n a fair shake, Ranger."

"Then we have a deal. Mitch, we'll spend the night here, then light out for Mexico at sunup. That'll give you time to bury your pa. No matter what else he might have been, he *was* your father. You'll be sorry later, if you don't say a few words over his grave."

"I doubt that, but I'll go along," Mitch said. "I am kinda surprised you don't want to leave right away. If we headed out now, we could cross the Rio before daylight, and hit the ranch at dawn."

"Ordinarily, I would, but there's three reasons I'm not, at least in this case. First, me'n Sarah Jane's horses need rest and a good feedin'. Second, so do we. Third, if I'm a new gunhand you're supposed to be escortin' to the place, it'd look awful suspicious if we showed up at first light. This way, we can all get a good night's sleep, take the entire day to reach your Mexican ranch tomorrow, and be ready for whatever happens when we get there. It's also a lot safer crossin' the Rio Grande in the daylight. The currents can be tricky, and there's quicksand to watch out for. Easier to avoid that durin' the day. Mitch, is there a room in the house Sarah Jane can use tonight? I'll be sleepin' in the bunkhouse."

"There's no need for you to do that, Ranger. We have several extra bedrooms in here."

"I appreciate the offer, but I've got a good reason for spendin' the night in the bunkhouse.

Just in case anyone gets the bright idea of ridin' on ahead of us to warn your brothers we're comin', I'll hear him. I also now realized, I never gave you my name. It's Luke Caldwell. My sister's is Sarah Jane Brundage."

Mitch introduced the rest of the Rocking W hands.

"If you're ready, Mitch, I'll have your father's body removed to the hay shed for the night," Mittler said. "Cookie has some stew left from supper keepin' warm on the stove, so I'll let him know there'll be two extra mouths. That is, as long as you don't mind eating in the bunkhouse dinin' room, Mrs. Brundage."

"Not at all. And please, call me Sarah Jane."

"Certainly. Jinx, Morty, take care of Mr. Williams. Ed, I want you and Quinn to dig his grave, out yonder by the big patch of prickly pear. He always liked seein' those bloom in the spring. Once that's done, we can all get back in our bunks, unless there's somethin' else you need, Ranger."

"Just where to put up our horses for the night, and where to get 'em some feed."

"I'll take you to the horse barn, show you where to put your cayuses, and stow your gear. I'll get some grain and hay for 'em while you do that."

"That'll be fine. Sarah Jane, there's no need for you to come along," Luke said. "I'll bring you your saddlebags, then take care of Casey for you."

"If you don't mind, Luke, I'd rather see to Casey myself. I can find my way back to the house just fine."

"You won't have to do that," Mitch offered. "I'll tag along while you see to your mount, then walk you back to the house. That is, unless you feel that would be improper . . . Sarah Jane."

"I believe that will be fine," Sarah Jane answered. "After all, my brother and I are putting our lives in your hands. I'm certain I'll be safe coming back here with you."

"Thank you. I'd imagine you've had a long day, and would like to freshen up before your dinner. Shep, I'd appreciate it if you would bring Sarah Jane's food up to the house. If there's enough, bring me a plate too."

"Sure, Mitch. Ranger, if y'all are ready, let's get your horses settled."

Luke lay awake, staring at the ceiling for some time before finally drifting off. Had he made the right decision, trusting Mitchell Williams? There was no denying the man hated his father, that was plain. What wasn't so plain was whether he hated his brothers just as much. Perhaps he wanted to protect them, so was leading Luke and Sarah Jane into a trap. Perhaps Hutch and Mace hated their father every bit as much as their brother

261

did, so Mitch had taken the opportunity to kill his father, and was planning to take Luke and Sarah Jane straight to their deaths, eliminating two witnesses, including the only one who could testify against his brothers. Or perhaps he would make certain both his brothers died facing arrest, then try and kill Luke and Sarah Jane, obtaining all of the Rocking W for himself. Whatever happened tomorrow, Luke had to be ready for it.

He rolled over onto his stomach, buried his face in his pillow, and fell into an uneasy slumber.

Chapter 14

The next day, Luke set an easy but steady pace as he, his sister, and Mitch rode south toward Mexico. Mitch was mounted on a well-muscled white gelding he called Spook.

"That's some horse you've got there, Mitch," Luke said.

"Yep, he sure is," Mitch agreed. "My father got him for me, down in Coahuila. Said he traded an old Mexican farmer a couple of prime heifers for Spook. I've always wondered whether he really traded with the *hombre* for him, or just forced the old man to hand him over. That'd be more typical of the way my father worked."

"You mind if I ask you a few questions, Mitch?"

"Not at all. If I don't like 'em, I just won't answer 'em."

"That's fine. First, are you the youngest in your family?"

"No, I'm the middle brother. Hutch is two years older'n me, and Mace three years younger. We had a baby sister, but she died less'n a month after she was born. Whatever spirit my mother still had died with little Ellen. She quit tryin' to stand up to my father, and spent most of the time in her room."

"I'm sorry. Why didn't she ever try to leave?"

"She had nowhere to go. Her family had all passed on, and Pa never let her have any money of her own. Hell, he never even let her go into town unless one of us boys, or one of the hands, went with her."

"Did you ever think of just pullin' up stakes and leavin'?"

"Plenty of times. In fact, when I was about twelve, I did run off. My Pa had some of his men run me down and drag me back home. He beat me so bad I thought he'd killed me, but I pulled through. After that, yeah, I thought about leavin', but just didn't have to guts to do it. My Pa would've just tracked me down again anyway, and then he damn sure would've killed me. I just stuck it out, best as I could, waitin' for my chance to break loose. Turns out you and your sister were it."

"Did you know what your father and brothers were doin'?"

"You mean robbin' and swindlin' people, forcin' folks off their land, burnin' them out if they wouldn't sell? Sure, I knew it. I even figured they killed some folks, although I never had any proof. But I for certain never thought they'd go in for killin' lawmen, and rapin' women. My apologies, Sarah Jane. Mebbe if I weren't such a coward, your husband might still be alive, and you wouldn't have been attacked so viciously by my brothers."

264

"There's no need to apologize to me," Sarah Jane answered. "You had nothing to do with your family's crimes. As far as being a coward, I don't see where you had much choice, under the circumstances. And you were certainly brave last night. I'm sorry for you, having to kill your own father."

"You needn't be. Sooner or later, either he was gonna kill me, or me him. I don't have any regrets over sending that rotten son of a bitch straight to the Devil."

"Mitch, does either of your brothers ride a *flaxen-maned* sorrel or chestnut?" Luke asked.

"Yeah, Mace does. A copper sorrel with a flaxen mane and tail. Why?"

"Because I found a piece of flaxen horsehair where the men who killed Hank left their horses. That'll help place Mace at the scene. Either of 'em own a black saddle, trimmed with fancy silver and turquoise *conchos*?"

"That'd be Hutch's rig. He got it from a Mexican saddlesmith in Zaragoza. Did someone recognize his saddle?"

"No, his horse must've gotten itchy, and rubbed against a mesquite. I found a silver and turquoise *concho* lyin' in the dirt where the horse had been tied, and some shreds of black leather stuck in the mesquite's bark. I've got those, along with the hair from Mace's horse, wrapped in oilcloth in my saddlebags. Those pieces of evidence will help nail your brothers. Once I get my hands on Hutch's saddle, if it's missin' a *concho* that matches the one I found, it'll prove he was at my sister's house the day of Hank's murder, along with your other brother."

"I hope you're right, Luke. My brothers are more slippery'n a sack of snakes, though. They're liable to wiggle out of any trap you set."

"I hope, with your help, to set a trap they *won't* wriggle out of," Luke answered. "I'm assuming you know the lay of the land around your Mexican ranch, right?"

"I sure do."

"Good. Will there be any guards posted?"

"There's usually one or two at the main gate. The house, bunkhouse, and horse stable are surrounded by an adobe wall, around four feet high, and a foot thick. There's no good cover for a quarter mile around the place, so you can be certain we'll be seen before we ride in."

"You think you'll be able to talk us past those guards?"

Mitch shrugged.

"*Quien sabe*? I would think so, since I know most of the men down there. But, if my brothers have any of the gunfighters they took along watchin' the gate, I can't say for certain."

"Let's hope you can. Otherwise, we'll have to take care of those guards, without anyone noticin' until we get inside the house."

"I'll do my best."

"*Bueno*. How many hands are there around the place?"

"About thirty *vaqueros*. There's a Mexican woman who's the cook and housekeeper. We shouldn't have to worry about the *vaqueros*. They're not gunfighters, just *hombres* who work with the cows and horses. It's the gunhands that concern me."

"How many of them do you think there are?"

"About a dozen, give or take. Adding in my brothers means we'll be outnumbered more'n six to one."

"Not bad odds for a Texas Ranger," Luke answered, with a grim chuckle.

"They're not as bad as you think, Mitch," Sarah Jane added. "I'm in this fight too. That makes the odds more like four to one."

"And if we can capture your brothers without any gunplay, those hired guns most likely won't give us any trouble," Luke said. "Once they see the risk of losin' their lives is bigger'n collectin' their wages, most men like those'll just up and leave. They'd rather fight dirty, preferably doin' their killing from ambush. Listen, I figure we're about two hours from the border. We'll stop here for a spell, to give the horses a breather, and ourselves a rest. We can palaver some more while we eat and smoke."

Chapter 15

Luke and his companions neared the Williamses' Mexican ranch about ninety minutes before sundown. They paused just before reaching the entrance.

"There's two men watchin' the gate," Mitch said. "Appears like they've already spotted us."

"You recognize either of 'em?" Luke asked.

"I dunno their names, but they look like two of the gunhands my father sent down here with my brothers."

"You reckon we'll have a problem gettin' past 'em?"

"*Quien sabe*? They should let me pass, but I wouldn't put any money on it."

"I sure hope they do," Luke said. "From the looks of the place, it'll be a helluva job tryin' to shoot our way in there, if it comes to that. Sarah Jane, this is where I have to tell you to stay back, and where you tell me there's not a snowball's chance you will. So let's just say we did, and get that over with."

"It'll save time," Sarah Jane answered, smiling.

"What about the *hombres* in the bunkhouse, Luke?" Mitch asked.

"Gunhands like your pa hired wouldn't stay in a bunkhouse, especially with a bunch of Mexican *vaqueros*," Luke answered. "The men we want will be in the main house. As far as the *vaqueros*, I'm sure they won't want any part of this fight. We shouldn't have to worry about them."

"I hope you're right."

"There's only one way to find out. Let's head on in, and see what happens."

Luke put his horses into a slow walk, with Mitch on his left and Sarah Jane on his right. When they reached the gate, one of the guards signaled them to stop.

"Hold it right there. Who are you, and what's your business here?' he asked. He took the rifle he held across his chest and aimed it at Luke's belly.

"I'm Mitchell Williams, one of the owners of this spread," Mitch answered him. "My father sent me down here with another man to help run the damn Mexes off. This here's him."

Mitch jerked a thumb in Luke's direction.

"Is that so? What's your name, Mister?"

"Luke."

"You got a last name to go with that?"

"Smith. Or Jones. Take your pick."

"Oh, yeah. Tommy, seems like we've got a real wise mouth on our hands."

"Seems so, Burt. Who's that with you, Mr. Smith or Jones?"

"My kid brother, Sammy. Don't let his looks fool you, though. He's better with a gun than most men twice his age."

"I reckon we'll just have to see about that."

Tommy started to reach for his gun.

"Hold it right there," Mitch ordered. "My pa'd be none too happy if one of you jugheads got killed just because your back is up. All of you, cool off. Just let us on through, and there'll be no trouble."

"Not so fast, *hombre*," Burt answered. "Nobody said anythin' about another man bein' hired, plus Hutch and Mace sure didn't mention havin' another brother. I didn't see you at the Rocking W, either. Do you recollect seein' him, Tommy?"

"No, I sure don't. I reckon we'd better check with one of the Williams brothers, to make certain he is who he claims to be. You got a problem with that, Mister?"

"Not at all. My brothers will tell you who I am."

"Go ahead, Tommy," Burt said. "If any of these *hombres* makes a wrong move, I'll plug him."

"We're not lookin' to stir up trouble," Mitch said.

"I'll be right back, Burt."

Tommy swung into his saddle, turned his horse, put it into a gallop, and headed for the house.

"You mind if we roll a smoke while we're waitin'?" Luke asked.

"Go ahead. Don't make any sudden moves, though."

"Don't plan on it."

Luke and Mitch took out the makings, rolled and lit quirlies.

"How come your kid brother didn't roll a smoke?" Burt asked.

"He ain't got his growth yet," Luke answered. "Don't want him to turn out stunted."

"He don't talk much, neither."

"I let my guns do the talkin' for me," Sarah Jane answered.

Burt laughed.

"Oh, is that so, sonny boy? That's somethin' I'd be plumb tickled to see. Hell, your voice ain't even changed yet."

"You just might get your chance."

"We'll see about that later. Looks like your brothers are comin' out, Mr. Williams," Burt said, with a sneer.

Hutch and Mace had stepped onto the veranda. Mitch was wearing a patch over his left eye. Both his cheeks bore long scars. The brothers looked closely at the three newcomers.

"Mitch, what the hell are you doin' down here in Mexico?" Hutch shouted. "We ain't had no word from Pa about any new men."

"He figured he didn't need to send word since I was comin' along," Mitch answered. "You on the prod, brother? You don't seem all that happy to see me."

"We're not," Mace answered. "You were always one to run from a fight, not look for one.

It don't make sense, you comin' down here. Who'd you say that was with you?"

"I didn't, but his name's Luke Smith. His kid brother is Sammy."

"I dunno, Mitch," Mace said. "There's somethin' awful familiar about that stockin'-footed bay the kid's forkin'. I've seen that horse somewhere before."

"There's lots of stockin'-footed bays in Texas," Mitch said.

"I dunno, either. The rider's what's botherin' me. I've seen him someplace, too," Hutch said. "Ride in closer so we can get a better look, Mitch."

"Sure, Hutch."

Before Mitch could start his horse moving, Sarah Jane took off her hat, letting her hair fall loose.

"You should recognize me, you damn bastard. You and your brother both. Do you remember me now?"

"Dammit!" Hutch cursed. "It's you. The woman from Sonora. Brundage's wife. We thought you were dead."

"You thought wrong." Sarah Jane pulled out her six-gun and took a hasty shot at Hutch, which punched a hole through the side of his shirt.

"Aw, hell!" Luke exclaimed, as the Williams brothers grabbed for their guns. He yanked his Winchester from its boot and fired a quick shot at Tommy, hitting him in the chest. Sarah Jane shifted her pistol and put a bullet through Burt's stomach.

"I told you I let my guns talk for me," she said, as Burt dropped his rifle, clutched his middle, and slumped against the wall.

"Get off your horses and behind cover," Luke ordered, as shots began seeking them out from the house. He fired several more shots in the direction of the Williams brothers, then rolled off Pete and ducked behind the wall. Pete and RePete trotted off, away from danger. Sarah Jane and Mitch dove from their horses and huddled in the wall's shelter, on the other side of the gate.

Tommy had fallen on his back, halfway through the door, when Luke shot him. Realizing they were exposed to the Ranger's and his companions' guns, Hutch and Mace jumped over his body and inside the house. Another gunman appeared in the doorway. He fired several times to keep Luke and his partners pinned down, then attempted to pull his dead partner inside. Luke put two bullets into his gut. The man jackknifed, and collapsed across Tommy. Luke fired several more shots through the door.

"Mitch, keep firin' at that door," he yelled, as he reloaded his rifle. "Make certain no one drags those bodies outta the way and gets it shut. That's the only way we have of gettin' inside that house."

"I'll take care of it, Luke."

Men appeared at the house's windows, punching out the glass and sending a volley of lead at Luke and his partners.

"Hold it, all of you!" Hutch bellowed. "Let's just see what's goin' on here. Mitch."

"Yeah, Hutch?"

"What the hell is this all about?"

"It's about finally gettin' the guts to stand up to you and Pa."

"You'd better explain that. Pa'll be some unhappy to find out you've gone up against your own family. He'll take a bullwhip to you and slice you to ribbons. So go ahead, talk. I'm listenin'."

"Pa won't hurt anyone ever again," Mitch answered. "He's dead."

"What'd you say? Pa's dead?"

"He sure enough is. I killed him."

Alongside Hutch, Mace snorted.

"You expect us to believe that? You, who has a yellow streak a mile wide up your spine? You haven't got the guts."

"He tried to kill me and my friends here, so I killed him. Simple as that. Now we're gonna kill you."

"Fat chance," Mace said.

"Mitch, you keep shut a minute," Luke ordered. "All you in the house, too."

"Who exactly are you, Mister?" Hutch asked.

"I'm Lieutenant Luke Caldwell, Texas Rangers.

You and your brother are under arrest for the murder of Sonora Marshal Hank Brundage, as well as assault, rape, and attempted murder of his wife. I'm askin' you to surrender peaceably."

Hutch gave a derisive laugh.

"Are you plumb loco, Ranger? This house is built like a fort, to protect against Apache and Yaqui attacks. And we've got you way outnumbered. You'll never get to us. Your only hope, all three of you, is to ride on back to Texas, and hope we don't catch up to you before you cross the Rio."

"A Ranger don't quit a trail. You know that, Williams. Either give yourselves up, or we'll come in after you. The rest of you men in the house, listen to me. The men you're working for are wanted on a bunch of charges. The worst are murder of a peace officer, then raping his wife, and beating her almost to death. Hank Brundage, the man they killed, was a former Ranger, my ridin' pard and good friend. He was also my brother-in-law. The woman they raped and beat so badly is my sister. As you heard, she's here with me and Mitch Williams today. I don't expect any of you to give a damn about Hank's murder, but do you really want to work for men who would mistreat a woman so badly? I'll give y'all five minutes to think about that, and make up your minds. If you decide you want out, I'll let you ride away, no questions asked. But I'm takin' the Williams brothers in, one way or the other. As far as bein' outnumbered, mebbe. But you're goin' up against a Texas Ranger, who would like nothin' better than to gun down the Williamses and everyone in there with 'em, but is sworn to uphold the law and dispense justice, not vengeance, much as I'd like to forget that, then Mitch Williams, a man who has finally found the guts to stand up to the father who killed his mother, and along with his other sons abused Mitch for years. Finally, probably the most trouble as far as you fellers are concerned, you're facin' a woman who watched her husband, who saw her bein' raped, but couldn't do a thing to help her, since he'd been stabbed in the belly and pistol whipped over the head, die slow and painful. She's mad as hell, and nothin's gonna stop her from gettin' her revenge, not even me. I don't know how much you men are bein' paid, but it's nowhere near the incentive the three of us have for seein' y'all dead. You've got five minutes."

"We don't need five minutes," someone shouted. "We're bein' paid real well, and we ain't about to walk away from that kind of *dinero*. We'll blast you to Hell."

"Suit yourself," Luke answered. He rose to one knee, and snapped off a shot. A man in one of the windows gave a short scream of pain as Luke's bullet plowed through his forehead and into his brain. An answering hail of lead from the house drove Luke back into cover. Chips of adobe went flying in all directions when the bullets slammed into the wall.

For several minutes, shots were exchanged, to no effect. Then, four men appeared at the front corners of the house, firing as they ran. Luke dove onto his belly in front of the open gate, levering and triggering his rifle as rapidly as possible, while bullets sought him out. He downed two of the men before they were halfway across the yard. The third took Luke's bullet in his belly, but kept coming, until Sarah Jane shot him in the chest, spinning him to the ground. The fourth man shot Luke in the side, then a bullet from Mitch tore through the gunman's throat, severing his jugular. With a fountain of blood spraying from his neck, the man collapsed. Luke rolled back behind the wall.

"How bad are you hit, Luke?" Mitch yelled.

"I dunno, but it hurts like hell," Luke answered. "Are you two all right?"

"A couple slugs came close, but I'm not hit," Mitch answered.

"Me either," Sarah Jane said.

"Good. Listen, I've got an idea. Mitch, do you know how to get around the back of the house?"

"I sure do."

"You think you can make it that far, while I rush the front door? Then we can get inside and catch those *hombres* in a crossfire. That might be our only chance to win this thing."

"I'm pretty sure I can, yeah."

"What about me?" Sarah Jane asked.

"You'll need to keep us covered, and pin down those men as best you can. Once we're inside, you can stay out here and watch for anyone tryin' to run. If anyone does, drop him in his tracks."

"If no one does, I'll be comin' in to join you, little brother."

"I sure won't argue with you about that, Sis. Mitch, you ready?"

"Sure am."

"Then let's go. I'll give you two minutes head start."

"See you inside."

Luke and Sarah Jane kept up a withering fire, while Mitch circled around the house. Once he disappeared into the brush, Luke smiled at Sarah Jane.

"Time for me to go."

"You be careful, Luke."

"Always am. You do the same."

With his sister sweeping the house with bullets, Luke, running low and zig-zagging, raced for the front door. One bullet burned a path along his neck, another stung his left arm. He reached the door, jumped over the bodies blocking it, then dove to his belly, pumping four bullets into two men at the far end of the hallway. He tossed aside his empty rifle and took his Peacemaker from its holster. From somewhere in the back of the house, he could hear shouts, curses, and gunfire.

"Sounds like Mitch made it," he muttered. Another gunman appeared in a doorway. He and Luke fired at the same time, the gunman's bullet burning a path along Luke's ribs, Luke's taking the gunman in the center of his chest.

"Where's those damn Williamses?" Luke said to himself, as he searched the front rooms. He took a quick look at several bullet riddled bodies, but none were Hutch or Mace. There was no sign of Jody, either.

The gunfire from the back of the house had just about stopped when Luke reached the kitchen. A man matching Jody's description was hiding behind the overturned table, drawing a bead on Mitch's back.

"Hold it right there," Luke shouted. Startled, Jody jumped up and whirled. Luke shot him through the stomach, just as Mitch, now aware of the hidden killer, turned and put two bullets into Jody's back.

"*Gracias*, Luke," he said.

"*Por nada*," Luke answered. "Anyone still movin' in here?"

"Not unless you missed somebody," Mitch answered. He grinned, then wiped away the blood running down his forehead and into his eyes.

"You seen any sign of your brothers?" Luke asked.

"No. You?"

"Nope. Don't see how they could've gotten past us. They've gotta be around here somewhere. We've got to find 'em."

The crash of shattering glass came from a locked side room, then footsteps running across the yard, followed by a flurry of shots.

"Sarah Jane!" Luke exclaimed. He and Mitch raced for the front door. Lying in front of the house was Mace, writhing in pain, from a bullet which Sarah Jane had put in his right side. The slug had entered between two ribs, passed upwards through his abdominal cavity, and exited just under his left armpit. He only had a few minutes to live. In the middle of the yard, Hutch stood stock still, staring at the rifle Sarah Jane held pointed at him.

"You killed my husband, damn you," Sarah Jane shouted. "Now it's your turn."

"Sarah Jane, don't," Luke called.

"After what this bastard did to me?" Sarah Jane answered. "You expect me to just let him walk away? I'm not about to let that happen, little brother."

"Sarah Jane, think. Don't do this," Luke pleaded. "Let a judge and jury hang him, nice and legal-like."

"I can't take the chance he'll buy some fancy talkin' lawyer who'll get him off, scot-free."

"Lady, listen to your brother, please," Hutch begged. He was shaking, sweat pouring down his face. "Don't shoot me. You'll never forgive yourself if you do."

"I'll take that chance."

"Ranger, talk some sense into your sister," Hutch cried. "You're a lawman. You can't just let her shoot down a man in cold blood."

"Give me one good reason why, after what you did to her."

"Because you're sworn to uphold the law, that's why."

"Funny time for you to care about the law," Luke answered. "But he's right, Sarah Jane. Let me handle him. Put down your gun."

"I . . . I don't know," Sarah Jane said. "I guess . . ."

She started to lower her rifle. When she did, Hutch lunged at her. Before he made three steps, Sarah Jane shot him in his groin. He grabbed his crotch, dropped to his knees, then toppled onto his side and doubled up, whimpering.

"Damn!" Mitch said. "She blew his balls clean off."

"Give me the rifle, Sis," Luke said. "It's over." She nodded, then handed him the weapon.

"Are you gonna be all right?"

"Yes. Yes I am. Shootin' that son of a bitch will

never bring back what he took from me, but it sure felt good."

Hutch was still whimpering, tears rolling down his cheeks.

"Why'd you help these people, Mitch?" he asked.

"Partly because of my conscience, for not goin' to the law about you, Mace, and Pa sooner," Mitch answered. "And partly for myself. I finally found the guts to be a man, and do what was right."

Blood was soaking Hutch's whipcord pants. Apparently, Sarah Jane's bullet had severed a major artery in his right leg.

"Never expected . . . this," he half-whispered, then exhaled his last breath.

Sarah Jane and Mitch were both bleeding from several wounds, as was Luke.

"Can you two make it across the Rio before we patch ourselves up?" Luke asked.

"We sure can," Mitch answered.

"Good. Then let's get outta here before the *Rurales* come snoopin' around. You got someone who can take charge here, Mitch?"

"I do. Felipe!"

At Mitch's call, a slim young Mexican emerged from the bunkhouse.

"*Sí, Señor* Williams?"

"Me and my friends have got to return to Texas. I'm now the sole owner of the family's property.

I'm placing you in charge. Bury the bodies, and clean up the place. I'll get back as soon as possible. When the *Rurales* show up, tell them the truth."

"*Sí, Señor.* I will do that."

"*Gracias*, Felipe. *Adios*."

"*Vaya con Dios, Señors and Señora.*"

Chapter 16

Luke and Sarah Jane spent several days at the Rocking W, recuperating from their wounds and getting some much needed rest. Luke sent a telegram to Ranger Headquarters with a brief explanation of what had occurred, then a second to his wife that he and Sarah Jane were safe, and would be home shortly. He followed those up with a full written report to Austin. Now, they were preparing to leave.

"Thanks again for all your help, Mitch," Luke said. "I don't know if I could have gotten this done without your help."

"And Sarah Jane's," Mitch answered, smiling at her.

"That's right," Luke agreed.

"And thank *you,* Mitch," Sarah Jane said. She kissed him on the cheek. Mitch blushed bright crimson.

"I reckon we'd better hit the trail. I want to cover a lot of miles before dark," Luke said. "Mitch, if you need anythin' else, especially when dealing with the Mexican authorities, you just let me know."

"I'll do that."

Mitch looked at the ground, turned his hat in his hands, and shuffled his feet. Finally, he looked at Luke's sister.

"Sarah Jane," he said, swallowing hard. "I realize this is a bit forward of me, and it's far too soon; however, once your period of mourning is over, if I happen to be up Sonora way, would you do me the honor of allowing me to call on you? Strictly socially, of course."

"Why, that would be very sweet, Mitchell. Of course you may. Just don't take too long. I'm not the kind of woman who can spend an entire year in black crepe and crinoline, mourning."

"But what would people say, especially the society ladies? Think of your reputation."

"The hell with society," Sarah Jane said. She laughed. "Besides, what little reputation I did have is long gone by now."

"Then it will be all right? I have your brother's permission to perhaps court you?"

"Not that you need it, but you have it," Luke answered. "It doesn't matter anyhow. If you haven't figured her out by now, my sister does what she damn well pleases."

"My brother's right. In fact, I just might apply for the deputy marshal's job when I get back home."

"See what I mean, Mitch?"

"I reckon I do."

"Good. Best of luck to you. Sarah Jane, let's go."

They swung into their saddles. Sarah Jane leaned down to give Mitch another kiss, then kicked Casey into a gallop. Luke had to urge Pete and RePete to match Casey's stride.

"*Adios*, Mitch," he called over his shoulder, waving.

"*Adios*," Mitch shouted back. He waved his hat over his head, then watched until Luke and Sarah Jane were out of sight.

About the Author

James J. Griffin, while a native New Englander, has been a lifelong horseman, and student of the Old West, particularly the Texas Rangers. He is considered an amateur historian of the Rangers, and has worked for many years in collaboration with the Texas Ranger Hall of Fame and Museum in Waco. He strives for historical accuracy in his writing, within the realm of fiction. Horses play a big part in Jim's stories, reflecting his love and knowledge of all things equine. He is a member of the Western Writers of America, Western Fictioneers, and a four time finalist for the Western Fictioneers Peacemaker Award. When not traveling out West, Jim makes his home in Keene, New Hampshire.

Center Point Large Print
600 Brooks Road / PO Box 1
Thorndike, ME 04986-0001 USA

(207) 568-3717

US & Canada:
1 800 929-9108
www.centerpointlargeprint.com